P9-EMK-200

# ONE COMANCHE
# TOO MANY

Charging on his pony, the Comanche fired his Colt. Fargo ducked. The Indian was half turned when Fargo flung the tomahawk and saw the heavy blade fly end over end and bury itself almost to the handle in the man's chest. The Indian's hands were still wrapped around the handle when he hit the ground.

Quickly Fargo turned to see another brave reaching out for the fallen Colt on the ground. Fargo started for the brave, but saw he was too late as the man's hand closed on the gun. And all Fargo could do was curse as the gun came up . . .

Ⓢ **SIGNET WESTERNS BY JON SHARPE** (0451)

# RIDE THE WILD TRAIL

☐ THE TRAILSMAN #68: TRAPPER RAMPAGE (149319—$2.75)
☐ THE TRAILSMAN #69: CONFEDERATE CHALLENGE (149645—$2.75)
☐ THE TRAILSMAN #70: HOSTAGE ARROWS (150120—$2.75)
☐ THE TRAILSMAN #71: RENEGADE REBELLION (150511—$2.75)
☐ THE TRAILSMAN #72: CALICO KILL (151070—$2.75)
☐ THE TRAILSMAN #73: SANTA FE SLAUGHTER (151399—$2.75)
☐ THE TRAILSMAN #74: WHITE HELL (151933—$2.75)
☐ THE TRAILSMAN #75: COLORADO ROBBER (152263—$2.75)
☐ THE TRAILSMAN #76: WILDCAT WAGON (152948—$2.75)
☐ THE TRAILSMAN #77: DEVIL'S DEN (153219—$2.75)
☐ THE TRAILSMAN #78: MINNESOTA MASSACRE (153677—$2.75)
☐ THE TRAILSMAN #79: SMOKY HELL TRAIL (154045—$2.75)
☐ THE TRAILSMAN #80: BLOOD PASS (154827—$2.95)
☐ THE TRAILSMAN #82: MESCALERO MASK (156110—$2.95)
☐ THE TRAILSMAN #83: DEAD MAN'S FOREST (156765—$2.95)
☐ THE TRAILSMAN #84: UTAH SLAUGHTER (157192—$2.95)
☐ THE TRAILSMAN #85: CALL OF THE WHITE WOLF (157613—$2.95)
☐ THE TRAILSMAN #86: TEXAS HELL COUNTRY (158121—$2.95)
☐ THE TRAILSMAN #87: BROTHEL BULLETS (158423—$2.95)
☐ THE TRAILSMAN #88: MEXICAN MASSACRE (159225—$2.95)
☐ THE TRAILSMAN #89: TARGET CONESTOGA (159713—$2.95)
☐ THE TRAILSMAN #90: MESABI HUNTDOWN (160118—$2.95)
☐ THE TRAILSMAN #91: CAVE OF DEATH (160711—$2.95)
☐ THE TRAILSMAN #92: DEATH'S CARAVAN (161114—$2.95)
☐ THE TRAILSMAN #93: THE TEXAS TRAIN (161548—$3.50)
☐ THE TRAILSMAN #94: DESPERATE DISPATCH (162315—$3.50)
☐ THE TRAILSMAN #95: CRY REVENGE (162757—$3.50)
☐ THE TRAILSMAN #96: BUZZARD'S GAP (163389—$3.50)

Prices slightly higher in Canada

---

Buy them at your local bookstore or use this convenient coupon for ordering.

**NEW AMERICAN LIBRARY**
P.O. Box 999, Bergenfield, New Jersey 07621

Please send me the books I have checked above. I am enclosing $_____
(please add $1.00 to this order to cover postage and handling). Send check or
money order—no cash or C.O.D.'s. Prices and numbers are subject to change
without notice.

Name_____

Address_____

City _____ State _____ Zip Code _____
Allow 4-6 weeks for delivery.
This offer is subject to withdrawal without notice.

# THE TRAILSMAN 97

# QUEENS
# HIGH BID

by

## Jon Sharpe

A SIGNET BOOK

**NEW AMERICAN LIBRARY**

A DIVISION OF PENGUIN BOOKS USA INC.

## PUBLISHER'S NOTE

This is a work of fiction. Names, characters, places, and incidents either are the product of the author's imagination or are used fictitiously, and any resemblance to actual persons, living or dead, events, or locales is entirely coincidental.

NAL BOOKS ARE AVAILABLE AT QUANTITY DISCOUNTS
WHEN USED TO PROMOTE PRODUCTS OR SERVICES.
FOR INFORMATION PLEASE WRITE TO PREMIUM MARKETING DIVISION,
NEW AMERICAN LIBRARY, 1633 BROADWAY,
NEW YORK, NEW YORK 10019.

Copyright © 1989 by Jon Sharpe

All rights reserved

Ⓢ

SIGNET TRADEMARK REG. U.S. PAT. OFF. AND FOREIGN COUNTRIES
REGISTERED TRADEMARK—MARCA REGISTRADA
HECHO EN DRESDEN, TN, U.S.A.

SIGNET, SIGNET CLASSIC, MENTOR, ONYX, PLUME, MERIDIAN
and NAL BOOKS are published by New American Library, a division of
Penguin Books USA Inc., 1633 Broadway, New York, New York 10019

First Printing, January, 1990

1 2 3 4 5 6 7 8 9

PRINTED IN THE UNITED STATES OF AMERICA

# The Trailsman

Beginnings . . . they bend the tree and they mark the man. Skye Fargo was born when he was eighteen. Terror was his midwife, vengeance his first cry. Killing spawned Skye Fargo, ruthless, cold-blooded murder. Out of the acrid smoke of gunpowder still hanging in the air, he rose, cried out a promise never forgotten.

The Trailsman they began to call him all across the West: searcher, scout, hunter, the man who could see where others only looked, his skills for hire but not his soul, the man who lived each day to the fullest, yet trailed each tomorrow. Skye Fargo, the Trailsman, the seeker who could take the wildness of a land and the wanting of a woman and make them his own.

*1860, west of Las Cruces,
in the New Mexico territory,
where the two most common things
were cactus and killing . . .*

# 1

The boy was running along the bank of the river, swerving, darting, trying to avoid the three horsemen who were chasing him. The big man on the magnificent Ovaro watched from a hillock, half-hidden by dry brush and chulla plants. He wasn't one to interfere without a good reason. The boy might be a runaway of some sort, he pondered. Lithe, dark-skinned, with black hair, undoubtedly Mexican, the boy was doing a good job of avoiding his pursuers. He'd let them almost reach him before darting away, and dropping low under a whirling lariat to double back on his tracks.

But he was tiring, the big man on the Ovaro noted, his movements less crisp, his turns slower. Skye Fargo leaned forward in the saddle as he watched. Had the boy stolen something? he wondered. The three men were intent on trying to catch him—there was nothing casual about their pursuit.

As he watched, one of the riders managed to swing his horse's rump around, and the young boy went sprawling onto his face at the edge of the river. He jumped to his feet instantly, but another of the men worked his horse in front of him, blocking his path. Again the boy swerved and darted to his left, avoiding the nearest rider only to be smashed to the ground by a swinging blow from the third rider, who leaned low from his saddle.

The boy again tried to push to his feet, but another of the men had leaned down and taken hold of him. The other two horsemen dismounted as the boy was yanked up by the neck. With narrowed, lake-blue eyes, Fargo scanned the boy's loose-fitting, Mexican peasant shirt, baggy pants, and sandals, and his handsome young features.

"Where is she?" Fargo heard one of the men ask as he shook the boy the way a dog shakes a bone.

"I don't know, *señor*," the boy said.

"The hell you don't, you little bastard." The man slapped the boy across the face. The boy fell to the ground but remained silent. He tried to scoot backward, but the man seized him again, flipped him around, and pushed him to the edge of the river. "You gonna answer me, goddammit?" the man snarled.

"I don't know," the boy said.

"Lying little bastard." The man shoved the boy into the water and pushed his head under the surface while the other two stood by. "Where is she?" he demanded again as he pulled the boy's head from the water.

Fargo watched the boy cough up water, struggling to take in air, as lines of fear and pain crossed his young face. "I don't know," he managed to cough out.

"One more chance," the man said as he pushed the boy's head underwater again. He held it there for almost half a minute and than yanked the boy up. The boy threw up more water, coughed and gagged, and struggled to escape from the man's grasp. He wasn't more than ten, Fargo guessed, and he was trying to summon the strength and resistance of a man.

"Drown the little bastard if he doesn't answer this time," one of the other men growled.

Fargo saw the boy glance up and blink, struggling to find courage while fear shone inside his brown eyes. The Trailsman grimaced. He had seen enough, and he reached down and drew the big Sharps from its saddle holster. He lifted the rifle to his shoulder and took aim.

"You gonna answer me?" the man said as he started to push the boy underwater again.

"Wait . . . wait," the boy choked. "I have to think."

Fargo half-smiled. The boy had guts. He was still playing for time. But the man wasn't inclined to wait, and he pushed the boy's head into the water. Fargo's finger pressed the trigger and the man's hat flew from his head.

"Jesus," the man snapped. He released his hold on the boy as he spun around and ducked just as Fargo fired again. This shot blew the hat off one of the other men, and Fargo lifted his cheek from the rifle stock.

"Keep your hands off the boy," he called as he spurred the Ovaro down the slope toward the river. Still holding the rifle ready to fire, he saw the three men look up and stare as he rode down to them. The boy sloshed out of the water and stood to the side, his round eyes wide.

"Who the hell are you?" the man who had held the boy underwater snarled. He had a round, beefy face with short-cropped hair, and he frowned at the intruder.

"That's not important," Fargo said. He lowered the rifle, pushing it into the saddle holster, while at the same time his right hand came to rest on the butt of the big Colt at his hip. "Why are you trying to drown the boy?"

"What the hell business is it of yours, mister?" one of the others muttered darkly.

"A not unreasonable question," Fargo conceded. "Let's say I don't like to see anybody drowned without one damn good reason. You have one?"

"We've been looking for this runaway bitch, and he knows where she is," the beefy-faced one said.

"I heard him say he didn't know," Fargo remarked.

"He's a little half-breed liar. He was on his way to town to buy food when we caught him with her purse."

Fargo tossed a glance at the boy and drew a shrug that was at least a halfway admission. "I still don't think that's reason enough to drown him," Fargo said to the man and saw the beefy face darken.

"You know, mister, I don't give a pig's ass what you think," the man said. "You got yourself off a couple of shots while we were busy. That's changed now. You've got five seconds to get your ass out of here, or you're never gonna poke your damn face into anything else again."

Fargo shrugged. "All right, but I'll take the boy with me," he said, and enjoyed the expression of astonishment that flooded the man's face.

"Goddamn, you must be plumb loco," the man said. "There are three of us."

"I can count," Fargo said calmly. The astonishment in the man's face gave way to a rush of uncertainty. Fargo knew the man was no gunhand, none of them was, and suddenly they were confronted by someone who defied the odds with icy disdain. The quick glances they exchanged were silent questions none of them wanted to answer. "We don't need to have any real trouble," the Trailsman said, focusing on the beefy-faced man. "You just get your hat before it floats away, and then you go on your way. Simple. No trouble."

12

"Sure," the man said. "Maybe that'd be best." He started into the water to retrieve his hat and Fargo cursed silently. He had caught the flash of craftiness that had come into the man's eyes. Fargo had concluded long ago that animals are smarter than men. They backed away from what they couldn't understand. They never felt the need to fight just to prove themselves smarter or craftier. He watched the man reach his hat where it floated on the surface. The man picked it up with his left hand as he whirled around and yanked out his six-gun. But the big Colt was already in Fargo's hand, the movement smooth and quick as a rattler's strike. The Colt barked, and the man's body arched backward, his chest exploding. He hit the water on his back, the red flow of blood instantly spreading.

The other two had used up their few precious seconds staring at their partner, and when they went for their guns, they found themselves staring at the big Colt leveled at them. Their hands froze in midair, then dropped to their sides.

"I'm glad you're not as dumb as he was," Fargo said. "Now take your guns out real slowly and drop them on the ground. Use two fingers only."

The men obeyed, unable to deny the fear they now felt.

"Now kick them over here," Fargo said, and they obeyed again. He swung from the Ovaro, bent down, emptied both guns, and left them on the ground. "Go get him and get out of here," Fargo said. "You can come back for your guns some other time."

The men nodded in unison, splashed into the red-stained water, and lifted the third man out. They carried him to his horse and draped him facedown across the saddle. Then they pulled themselves onto their own mounts and rode off without looking back. Only one word broke the silence.

"*Caramba!*" The word came on a half-hissing sound, and Fargo turned to look at the boy, who stared at him with round, wide eyes.

"Suppose you give me some answers," Fargo said sternly, and the boy nodded as he came closer. "You've a name?" Fargo asked.

"Miguel," the boy said.

"Who were you trying to protect?"

"My friend Verna."

"Tell me more."

"They were trying to bring her back."

"Who? Why? What's this all about?" Fargo frowned.

"Ed Benton's men. She has run away from him and he is very *enojado*," Miguel said.

"Why is he so angry?" Fargo questioned.

"She was housekeeper at his ranch. She ran the house, the kitchen, took care of all the buying. She was very important at Señor Benton's place. He says she cannot leave," Miguel said.

"But she ran away," Fargo offered, and Miguel nodded. "And you helped her," Fargo said, and the boy nodded again. "Why?"

"She is my friend. She helped me once. Now I help her."

"And almost get yourself killed for it," Fargo grunted.

"I'll take you to Verna if you will help her get away, *señor*," the boy said. "She will pay you, I'm sure."

"Were you going to town to get food when those three caught up with you?" Fargo asked.

"*Sí señor*," Miguel said, and drew a small cloth bag from his pocket. "Verna and I, we have been hiding for two days and we are hungry. I was only going to Mantilla."

Fargo nodded, letting his lips purse in thought. Mantilla was hardly a town. There were three buildings: a general store, a trading post, and a blacksmith. "I'll take you to Mantilla to get the food," Fargo said. "Then I'll see you get it to your friend. Swing up behind me."

"*Gracias, gracias*," Miguel said, and was in the saddle in one quick, lithe movement.

Fargo turned the horse to head down the slope toward Mantilla, less than a mile away. "Did you stay with your friend Verna at Benton's ranch?" he asked the boy.

"Yes, I help Verna, run errands for her, catch the chickens. I do many things," Miguel said, pride filling his voice.

"How old are you, Miguel?"

"Ten. Maybe nine," the boy said.

"In other words, you're not sure." Fargo smiled and felt Miguel's shrug. "Your working with your friend Verna, that was all right with Ed Benton?" Fargo had asked the question in an attempt to get a better picture of Ed Benton. So far he had only a ten-year-old's word about his friend Verna and her running away. Maybe there was a lot more Miguel didn't say or didn't really understand.

"Señor Benton never liked me helping Verna. He never liked me around the ranch," Miguel said. "Verna made him keep me around."

"Did you like him?" Fargo pressed.

"No. Señor Benton is very *áspero,*" Miguel said.

"Very rough, is he?" Fargo echoed, then fell silent.

The three buildings of Mantilla appeared, sunbaked and dusty, much like the rest of the New Mexico Territory. Fargo waited outside the general store while Miguel ran in and returned with a small bag of groceries.

"Biscuits and some dried-beef strips," Miguel said as he pulled himself onto the saddle.

"Which way?" Fargo grunted.

"To the river, where you saved me, then we go left into the hills," Miguel answered, and Fargo put the pinto into a trot.

He'd bring the boy back to Verna, he had decided, and be on his way. There were still far too many unexplained angles to the incident, and besides, he was due in Tablita in another day. At Miguel's directions, he turned into the hills after they reached the river, then turned again through a passage between high rocks and short, spineless bishop's cap cactus. They reached a hollow, and Miguel leapt to the ground.

"Verna," he called. "Verna." He turned, panic in his eyes. "She is not here," he said.

But Fargo's eyes were on the dusty trail outside the hollow. "She went that way," he said, letting the Ovaro follow the trail of footprints on the ground. They led down a passage, turned, then reached a wide place where the footprints were spread farther apart. She had run, Fargo decided, and then he saw the other prints, hoofmarks and bootprints. "She was caught here." he said.

"The others," Miguel said. "There were more than the three who chased me. I saw them."

"Why'd she leave the hiding place?" Fargo frowned.

"I think maybe because I was too long coming back. I tried to throw the ones chasing me off the track. She came out to look for me."

"A mistake," Fargo grunted.

"Now he has her back. Now she will never get away. He will not even let her go to Mantilla without a guard now," Miguel said. "I must go back to her."

"That's loyal, but maybe not too smart," Fargo said.

"Help her, *señor*. I know Verna will pay you," the boy pleaded.

Fargo fastened a sharp glance on the boy. "Why does she suddenly want to run away?"

"To find someone, a special man who she says will help her. That is all she told me," Miguel answered. "Please, *señor,* come with me. She is in trouble now."

Fargo made a face. The boy would go back on his own and try to save the woman. He was sure of that. The loyalty and caring shone deeply in his round eyes. "Climb on," he grunted.

*"Gracias! Gracias,"* Miguel said, and all but vaulted onto the saddle.

"No promises," Fargo said. "Show me the way to Benton's place."

As the boy gave directions, Fargo sent the Ovaro along a path of burr oak, and finally he saw the ranch spread in the distance. He turned and rode up onto a hill, moving as close to the ranch as he dared. His eyes swept the ranch. The main house was to the right, and had two corrals attached to it. One held a dozen scrawny longhorns, the other some forty hogs, mostly Poland China, none very well kept. A half-dozen hands went about their chores, and Fargo spotted a heavyset man talking to the two men who'd chased Miguel.

"Benton?" he murmured, and Miguel nodded. Fargo took in the man's face and saw a mouth that turned down at the corners in a heavy, crude frown. Benton went into the house and Fargo glanced at the sky: the long shadows of dusk were sliding downward. "It'll be dark in another hour. We'll wait here," he said to Miguel, and swung from the horse.

"Verna's room is the one in the corner, where the light just went on," Miguel said.

"Sit down. Learn to wait. It'll help you all through

**17**

life," Fargo said, and Miguel folded himself against a rock and fell silent.

Fargo's eyes swept the buildings below. The bunkhouse was some twenty yards from the ranch house, a stable sat five yards from the main building, and the corrals spread out to the rear. He dropped to one knee as dusk came. He saw Benton emerge from the house carrying a lantern and watched the man check a side door to make certain it was locked, then a rear door. He paused at each window, testing to see they were all locked.

"He's being extra careful," Fargo muttered. "His men no doubt told him they didn't know who I was. He's afraid Verna might have a new friend."

"She does, *señor*," Miguel said quickly.

"Maybe," Fargo said. He let almost another hour go by until he saw the light in the bunkhouse go out. He rose, then took the Ovaro's reins and led the horse almost to the bottom of the hill. He halted there, tied the reins loosely around a low branch, and moved forward, Miguel at his side.

The light was still on in Verna's room, and Fargo dropped to a crouch as he neared the window. The voices were clear enough through the closed window, and he halted at the sill and peered into the room. He saw Benton at one side, the man's back to him, and facing Benton was a young woman in a light-blue dress that clung to a somewhat thin figure. He took in her dark-brown hair and blue eyes. She had an attractive-enough face despite its thinness, with a straight nose and a very determined chin. Her very narrow waist seemed even smaller beneath well-shaped breasts that pulled the top of the dress tight.

"You've got no damn right to keep me here," Fargo heard the young woman say.

"I gave you a job and you're staying, girlie," Benton said.

"I didn't sign any contract. I didn't even promise you anything. You've no right."

"I don't give a damn about right. You're here until I kick your little ass out, and that's the way it is," Benton flung back. He moved a few paces to one side and Fargo saw the man's face flushed with anger. "Only, now there's going to be some changes around here. I'm keeping a rope and a guard with you until you promise to stop this damn-fool running away. And maybe I'll just do what I ought to have done with you long ago." Benton moved toward the young woman and Fargo saw Verna refuse to step back, though the whiteness in her cheeks was more from fear than defiance.

"Don't come any closer or I'll scratch your damn eyes out," Verna said.

Benton's hand movement was quick, a backhand slap that smashed into the girl's face. She stumbled backward and almost fell, but she managed to catch hold of the edge of a table.

Fargo felt more than saw the dark-skinned, lithe form next to him leap up, small fists doubled up to smash into the window. Fargo's hand shot out, seized him by the collar, and yanked him back and held him to the ground. "Be still," he hissed, never taking his eyes from the scene inside the room. He felt Miguel stand still beside him.

"You'll learn, girlie," Benton said as he strode to the door, yanked it open, and left the room.

Fargo saw the door slam shut and he heard the sound of a bolt being closed from the outside.

"What do we do now, *señor?*" Miguel whispered.

"He's locked the place up tight. He might have one of his boys inside as a guard," Fargo said.

"*Sí,* one of his men, Frank, is always in the house," Miguel said. "He sleeps on a chair in the hallway near Verna's room."

"Maybe we'd do best to wait for tomorrow. Benton might go off someplace and give us a chance to get in," Fargo said.

"I can get in now," Miguel said, and drew a glance of surprise from the big man at his side. Miguel motioned to him, and Fargo followed the small form along the side of the house, around the rear corner, where the boy halted alongside a small opening at the base of the wood. The hole was about two feet long and a little over a foot high, Fargo guessed. "It opens out from the kitchen," Miguel said. "There is no door to the outside from the kitchen. Water and cooking spills are swept out this way."

"You can fit yourself through there?" Fargo frowned. Miguel nodded, excitement and pride filling his small face. "What about Frank, the guard inside?" Fargo asked.

"I will go around the other hall," Miguel said.

"Go to the front door and let me in," Fargo said.

The boy nodded and Fargo watched with a combination of amazement and admiration as Miguel seemed to condense in front of his eyes. The boy knelt at the small opening, his shoulders drawn in, arms wrapped around his body, while at the same time he somehow stretched the lower part of his torso out almost snake-like. He crawled into the space headfirst, then continued to wriggle and twist until suddenly he disappeared inside the opening.

Fargo turned and moved carefully back around the house until he reached the front door. He waited impatiently and finally the door opened and he slipped into the darkened house. Miguel silently closed the door again and beckoned him down a hallway. The boy suddenly halted and Fargo saw the dark bulk of the guard seated in the chair tipped back against the wall. The man's head had dropped almost to his chest, and Fargo drew the Colt from its holster, holding it by the barrel as he moved on silent steps down the hallway. He brought the butt of the gun down on the man's head in a short, snapping arc and caught the figure before it fell to the floor. He lowered the limp form and pushed it against the wall while Miguel moved a half-step ahead of him and led the way to the door of Verna's room. He slid the bolt open and Fargo followed him into the room, where he saw the young woman sit up in a narrow cot along the wall.

"It's me," Miguel whispered, and Verna gasped in surprise. "And someone to help us escape," he added.

Verna swung from the cot, one hand held to the front of a white nightgown that dipped at the neckline to show the soft curves of her breasts. Fargo saw the questions form in Verna's eyes as she frowned at him, then glanced at Miguel.

"He saved me. He will save you," the boy said, and she returned her eyes to Fargo.

"This is no place to talk. Get dressed," Fargo said.

She turned away, her back to him as she stood in a corner of the room. She managed to shed the nightgown and put on the light-blue dress in one quick motion that let him see only the back of long, thin legs before she turned around.

"Get whatever things you want to take," he said.

She picked up a canvas sack. "It's all in here. I had it with me when they caught me. I didn't have time to unpack yet," Verna said.

"Let's go," Fargo said, and led the way from the room. He crept down the hallway and slipped out the front door, then halted outside, his eyes sweeping the darkness. "Go quietly into the stable," he said. "You're going to need a horse for yourself."

"And Miguel?" she asked as Fargo started for the stable.

"He's not big enough to handle a horse, and I don't want passengers if we have to run for it," Fargo said.

"There's a jenny inside he's ridden before," Verna said.

"Good enough. Get your mounts. Just lay the saddles on them. We'll tighten the cinches after we get away from here," Fargo said, and stepped to one side as the young woman and Miguel went into the stable.

Miguel came out first, leading a mule, and Verna followed a few moments later. "You know where I left my horse," Fargo said to Miguel. "Walk slowly toward the spot. Don't look around. Don't think about me."

The boy nodded and, with Verna following, he started across the open land near the corrals as Fargo dropped back into the dark shadows alongside the stable. It had gone smoothly so far, but he felt the misgivings curling inside himself. The guard inside the house could have come around by now and the soft clip-clop of the horse's hooves sounded inordinately loud in the silence.

Verna and Miguel were halfway across the open yard when Fargo caught the movement at the front door of the house. He drew the big Colt, waited, and saw a figure step from the house, clad in long johns, a rifle in his hand.

"That'll be far enough, bitch," Benton growled, and moved into the open, swinging the rifle around to fire.

Verna halted and Miguel moved to stand a few paces in front of her.

"Goddamn, you're gonna pay for this," Benton

rasped, and took another few steps closer. "First, I'm gonna blow that little bastard's head off for sneaking back and letting you out, though I don't know how the hell he got in. But it won't matter now. Then I'm gonna beat the hide off you so you won't ever think of sassing me back, girl."

Fargo, moving silently as a cougar on the prowl, came up behind Benton and halted a dozen feet from the man. "All you're going to do is put that rifle down," he said quietly, and Benton turned, surprise filling his face.

"Goddamn, you're the one Seth told me about," Benton said.

"You keep remembering what he told you and don't do anything stupid," Fargo said.

"You killed McGowan."

"His fault. I didn't want that. I don't want any more now," Fargo said.

"Then what the hell are you doing here?" the man rasped.

"I'm not sure," Fargo said. "But I'm taking the woman and the boy."

"The hell you are," Benton snarled.

Fargo heard the resignation in his voice as he spoke. "Don't make me do something I don't want to do. Just put the rifle down," he said.

It was too dark for Fargo to catch the changes in the man's eyes, so his gaze focused on Benton's hands. When he saw them tighten and begin to pull the rifle up another inch, he fired and saw the rifle fall as the bullet plowed into Benton's forearm.

"Ow, Jesus," Benton cried out, grabbing his arm with his other hand while the rifle hit the ground.

"Run," Fargo called.

Miguel and Verna obeyed and Fargo started to follow at a long-legged lope. He was more than halfway across the yard, Verna and the boy ahead of him, when he heard the voices. He spun to see the figures come out of the bunkhouse. He paused and fired the Colt, sending a spray of bullets toward the bunkhouse. The men dived back inside at once. He heard Benton screaming orders, but by the time his men emerged from the bunkhouse again, Fargo had reached the Ovaro. He saw Verna quickly tightening the cinch around her horse, then she helped Miguel adjust the cinch ring under the jenny. "Ride, we'll fix them better later," Fargo snapped as he climbed onto the Ovaro.

Benton's men wouldn't be chasing after them, he was certain. They'd be busy tending to their boss first, and it'd take them too long to dress and saddle up. But he set a fast pace up a long slope, then rode onto a flat ridge and continued north until he halted beneath a trio of cottonwoods.

"This'll do for the night," he said, and slid to the ground as Miguel and Verna tied their mounts to a low branch. He heard the boy talk quickly to the young woman in whispered tones.

Verna came forward as Fargo unsaddled the Ovaro, her tall figure held very straight, her eyes direct. "I hear we both owe you, mister," she said. "More than either of us can repay."

"Forget about that, but I'd like an explanation," Fargo said. "Why'd you have to run away suddenly?"

"I'd been thinking about leaving for a long time, but suddenly I have to get to Tablita to meet someone," Verna said.

"Tablita?" Fargo said, and found himself smiling. "Guess we'll be spending a little more time together. I was on my way to Tablita before I came onto Miguel."

"That's great," Verna said. "The world is full of

coincidences." Her smile burst forth suddenly, enhancing her beauty. "I think it's time I knew your name."

"Fargo . . . Skye Fargo," the big man said, and saw her eyes grow wide with surprise.

"The Trailsman?" Verna gasped.

"Some call me that."

"You're why I was going to Tablita—to find you, to talk to you, to hire you. I'll be damned," Verna exclaimed.

"I guess that makes two of us," Fargo murmured.

# 2

Fargo took in the flush of excitement that swirled through Verna's face, and he felt a nudge of unexplainable misgivings. "We've a lot to talk about," Verna said. Fargo cast a glance at the night sky and to where Miguel looked on in silence.

"I think we ought to save the talking for morning and get some sleep," Fargo said. "I'm sure Miguel will agree with that."

The boy half-shrugged, and Verna put her arm around his shoulder. "Yes, of course," she said. "I'm just so excited I've forgotten how tired I was a few hours ago. We'll talk tomorrow."

"I've an extra blanket," Fargo said as he took his bedroll down.

Verna took her sack of clothes and went behind one of the cottonwoods. Miguel had the blanket spread out by the time she returned wearing a short night-dress that showed her legs from the knees down—thin but strong, Fargo noted. Her modest breasts pushed the neckline of the nightdress out in soft twin mounds. She had a lean loveliness, he decided, a kind of spare beauty, and he watched her curl up on the blanket, almost into a little ball.

He undressed to his underdrawers, aware her eyes were on him. But when he turned, she had shifted and seemed asleep. He lay down and let sleep come quickly, aware that he was both curious and slightly apprehensive of the coming day.

When he woke with the new sun, Fargo had already decided to ask his own questions of Verna first. He rose, used his canteen to wash, and left it for Verna as he sauntered away from the three cottonwoods. He found a stand of rum cherry and carried a hatful of the fruits back for a sweet-tart breakfast.

Verna was dressed when he returned, her slender figure encased in worn Levi's and a tan shirt unbuttoned at the neck. She bent to pick up the blanket, and her small-waisted body moved with its own tight grace, her rear a little flat inside the Levi's, her breasts firm and hardly moving at all. But her eyes shone with new excitement as she returned the blanket to him, her face aglow with a lean attractiveness.

"Have some breakfast first," he said as she started to rush out a torrent of words. Miguel was first to scoop up a handful of the cherries and Fargo sat down and relaxed on one elbow. "Where did you and Miguel meet?" he asked.

"On the Mexican border," Verna answered. "Miguel was living with three older brothers and a sister when the Mexican army came by."

"They needed help in their barracks and they just came and took everyone. It is what they often do," Miguel said. "Only I ran. The army is very bad to people. They make slaves out of you."

"I was passing by in a surrey owned by an old couple I was working for. I stopped, Miguel jumped in, and I took off across the border with him," Verna said.

"With six *soldados* chasing us," Miguel put in.

"But I crossed over the border and the Mexicans stopped. They'd have crossed over after me but for a U.S. cavalry patrol riding within sight. They turned back, and Miguel's been with me since," Verna said.

"I will do anything for Verna. She saved me from becoming a slave for the army."

"How'd you come to meet Benton?" Fargo asked Verna.

"He advertised for a housekeeper and cook. I needed work, so I took it. Miguel came with me, of course. But Benton turned out to be a real bastard. He wanted more than a housekeeper, and I was wondering how much longer I could put him off."

Fargo nodded, pushed to his feet, and helped Verna up. "We'll talk more while we ride," he said, and he swung onto the Ovaro as Verna went to the gray and Miguel climbed atop the jenny.

Fargo led the way along a ridge and down a wide slope, the red pillars of sandstone like so many stone castles, each with its own buttresses. "How'd you know I'd be in Tablita?" Fargo asked.

"I heard you were going there to meet somebody," Verna said.

"Otis Frawley," Fargo supplied. "You said you were running away to hire me. Why?"

"You ever hear of Tom Yancey?" Verna asked.

"Everybody who's ever ridden through the Southwest has heard of Tom Yancey. To the law he was a bank robber, highwayman, outlaw, desperado. To others, he became a kind of folk hero, a sort of Robin Hood. There are all kinds of stories about Tom Yancey."

"I've one more," Verna said. "I met Tom Yancey before I went to work for Benton, before I met Miguel." Fargo felt his brows lift, but he searched her face and saw that she was completely serious. "I didn't

28

know who he was at first, but he was real sick and had been riding hard."

"Probably from a posse," Fargo commented.

"That's what he told me. He looked awful and had a high fever and terrible stomach pains. I had a small cabin and I put him up, took care of him, and nursed him back to being well enough to leave. He told me then that he was a sick man and how damn few people had ever helped him in anything and that he was really touched by what I'd done for him." She paused, alone in memories for a moment, then went on again. "He told me he had a lot of money hidden away, and if anything happened to him, he was going to give me a chance to get it. He stayed around a week more and I took care of him, and when he finally left, he told me I'd be hearing from him. I didn't really believe it."

"But you did hear from him," Fargo finished.

"A few weeks ago," Verna said. "I got this letter from a doctor in Silver City telling me that Tom Yancey had died and enclosing a note to me from Tom. The note said that if I could find his cabin, all the money he hid away could be mine."

"And you believe it," Fargo said.

"I sure do," Verna returned.

Fargo's smile was gentle. "You know, Tom Yancey had a reputation for the funny things he did. That helped make him into a folk hero for some people. Once he held up a stage, and instead of taking everyone's guns away as most bandits would, he took all their clothes. Another time, he arrived at a fancy barbecue a rich man was giving. After he took everybody's money and jewels, he made them all eat so much they could hardly move, much less chase after him."

"I know he was a strange man with a strange sense of humor, but this isn't an example of it. That's what you're thinking, isn't it?" Verna frowned and Fargo nodded. "No, there was no reason for him to send me the note unless he meant it. He was keeping his promise to me. He was really grateful."

"So you came to hire me to find the cabin for you," Fargo said.

"I hear you're the very best," Verna said.

"I'm already hired. Otis Frawley wants me to take a special herd a special way for him," Fargo told her.

"I'll pay you double whatever he's paying you," Verna said.

"I gave him my word. He's expecting me. You'll have to find somebody else."

"I don't know anybody else. Besides, this'll take someone special. I don't know where to begin," Verna returned.

"You don't even know if there is a cabin and any money in it."

"There is. Take my word for it," she snapped with the kind of conviction that let him think she had more reasons than the ones she'd given him.

"I'm sorry," Fargo said. "But I made an agreement with Otis. I won't break it."

"Not for a wild-goose chase," she sniffed angrily.

"Not for anything," he corrected and glanced at the boy. Miguel rode the mule with a serious expression on his small face, a furrow on his brow.

"We'll find somebody, Verna," the boy murmured consolingly, and Fargo saw the flat buildings of Tablita come into sight.

"If not, we'll try to find it ourselves," Verna said, glancing quickly at Fargo with reproof. "Meanwhile, we'll stay the night in Tablita and get you a change of clothes, Miguel."

Fargo fell silent and they rode beside him as he entered the town. Tablita was a town edging on respectability. The dance hall was still the center of its existence, but it boasted an inn and a general store. The first sizable town north of the border, it handled the trade of those coming or going from the new contours of the Mexican-American border. Most of the traders were trying to develop new business, but plenty of them were hard-eyed men looking only for a fast-and-easy dollar.

Fargo halted at the general store, and Verna's glance was a mixture of sulkiness and contrition. "I am grateful to you for what you did," she said. "I've no right to be angry."

"Forget it," he said. "If Otis hasn't arrived yet, I'll be staying at the inn. If Otis knows of somebody around who can help you, I'll leave the name with the desk clerk."

"Thanks," Verna said, and Fargo's eyes went to Miguel.

"You are a good man, *señor*," Miguel said with a smile.

"Don't overdo it," Verna sniffed.

"Good luck," Fargo said, and realized he felt sorry for Verna. Her determined, lean attractiveness bordered on desperation, but he knew that in all likelihood she was chasing an empty fable. From what he knew of Tom Yancey, it would be like the man to have a final laugh at the world. Verna may have misinterpreted his gratitude, he realized.

With a wave, he moved the pinto forward and felt Verna's eyes following him. He reached the inn, a modest, weathered building that advertised clean rooms and soft beds, and he dismounted and strode to a battered front desk. An elderly man in a green eyeshade looked at him with tired eyes. "My name's Fargo. I'm here to meet Otis Frawley. He check in yet?" the Trailsman asked.

31

"Nope," the man said. "But somebody else was asking for you."

"Somebody else?" Fargo frowned.

"Room Four," the man said. "Down the hall."

Fargo felt the furrow dig into his brow as he strolled the hallway to the last room, where a number four was only partly attached to the door. He knocked, the door opened, and he found himself staring at a young woman with thick, wild blond hair, a round face with light-blue eyes, full cheeks, and very red, full lips, all blending together to give a sensuous, pouty, and sultry attractiveness. "The desk clerk said someone in Room Four was asking for me. I'm Fargo," the Trailsman said.

The young woman's eyes widened at once. "Oh, great, come in, come in," she said, and Fargo stepped into a small room sparsely furnished with a cot, a dresser, and a single chair. "I'm Rosalie Hodges," she said, and he saw her eyes move across him with practiced experience. She wore a brown skirt, and deep large breasts strained the fabric of a dark-red cotton blouse. The rest of her matched, all a little overweight. She was pushing thirty, he decided.

"How'd you know I'd be here?" Fargo queried.

"Tom Terrent told me back in Yucca."

Fargo nodded. He'd told Tom he was coming to Tablita to meet Otis. "You've come a long way," he remarked.

"To find you," Rosalie said.

"Why?"

"I want to hire you. I need to find a cabin and I hear you're the best trailsman and scout there is," she said.

Fargo felt the furrow dig into his brow. "A cabin?" he echoed.

"That's right," Rosalie said. "You ever hear of Tom Yancey?"

The furrow grew deeper. "Yes. I'm getting to know all about Tom Yancey. You've something more to tell me about him?" Fargo asked cautiously.

"I sure do. I met Tom Yancey about a year ago. I was running a dance hall and I'd just closed up for the night when suddenly there he was. He had a leg wound and was bleeding badly. I took him in, treated his leg, and put him up. There were men looking for him, but nobody thought to look in a dance-hall house. It took two weeks before he was well enough to leave."

"He was real grateful to you for what you'd done, and he told you nobody ever helped him before," Fargo said blandly.

Rosalie frowned. "That's right," she said. "He told me he was a sick man and he might not have a lot longer to live. He said he'd a cabin hidden away and a lot of money, too. He said he'd give me a chance to get that money for what I did for him."

"And when he died, you got a letter from a doctor with a note in it from Tom Yancey telling you to find his cabin," Fargo said with a note of weariness.

Rosalie stared at him, surprise wreathing her round face, and she sank onto the edge of the lone chair. "How'd you know that?"

"Because somebody else just told me the same story," he answered, and her full red lips dropped open.

"No," she hissed. "That can't be."

"Only it is," he said, and suddenly felt sorry for Rosalie Hodges as shock clung to her face.

"The same story?" she echoed, still wrestling with disbelief.

"A few details were different. How she helped him was different, but that was all. The rest was pretty much the same. Her name's Verna Simpson," Fargo said. "You know her?"

"No, never heard of her," Rosalie said, and still stared at him in shock. But he saw her frown deepen and she flung shock aside and pushed to her feet. "Where is this Verna Simpson?" she asked.

"In town. I gave her the same answer I'm giving you. I've got a job to do," Fargo said.

"Goddamn, I don't believe this. I have to talk to her," Rosalie said angrily, her deep breasts lifting with a long sigh.

"I left her at the general store. There's a young boy with her. She's riding a gray with a white rump," Fargo said.

"I'll find her," Rosalie said, running one hand through the thick blond hair. "Dammit, I'll find out what she's trying to pull off here."

"Have fun," Fargo said as he followed her out of the room.

"This isn't fun," Rosalie shot back. "Tom Yancey didn't lie to me. He really was grateful for the way I helped him, and he didn't need to send me a note from his deathbed. He had a reason. He wanted to do something for me."

"He also had a twisted sense of humor. Maybe that's the reason for all this," Fargo said.

"No," she snapped with the same conviction he'd heard from Verna.

Fargo shrugged. "I still can't help you," he said, and Rosalie's round face frowned back at him.

"We'll talk more about that when I come back," she said, and hurried down the hallway, her ample rear jiggling as she stomped away.

He shook his head as he walked down the hall and watched her hurry outside. He felt sorry for her—for Verna, too, he realized—and he felt resentful of the late Tom Yancey for his strange sense of humor. But perhaps it was only in character. A man dies as he lives, Fargo reflected, and Tom Yancey had certainly lived a strange, bizarre life. This seemed but a last macabre gesture. The two young women would have to finally come to realize that, he grunted. He strode outside, untethered the Ovaro, and walked the horse to the south end of town.

Tablita had a public stable, and he paid the twenty-five cents to use their facilities and their equipment for a thorough grooming of the magnificent black-and-white stallion. He used the dandy brush first, the body brush to clean remaining dust from the coat, mane, and tail, the stable sponge for the snout and eyes, and finally the curry and stable rubber. The very last detail was to clean out the hooves, and when he was finished, most of the day had gone by. He walked the glistening horse back to the tethering post outside the inn and went to the front desk as dusk began to settle over town. "Otis Frawley come by yet?" he asked.

"Nope," the elderly man said.

"I'll take a room for the night," Fargo said. "Might as well enjoy a real bed while I'm waiting."

"Name?" the clerk said as he turned the registration book.

"You know the name." Fargo frowned.

"Need it official now," the man said primly.

"Fargo . . . Sky Fargo," the Trailsman grunted.

"Room Six," the clerk said, and handed him a single key.

Fargo returned to the Ovaro to grab his saddlebag. Dusk was quickly turning to night, he noted as he went back inside the inn, found the room, and put the lone lamp on low. He'd return to unsaddle the horse later, he decided, and he used the big porcelain basin on the dresser to wash.

All but naked, he lay down on the bed. A thorough grooming deserved a nap, he told himself, and let his eyes close. He knew only one thing when the knock on the door woke him—he hadn't napped for long. He swung his legs from the bed, pulled on trousers, and went to the door. He opened it to see a young woman standing there, brown hair cut short, light-brown eyes, a nice mouth, and a pretty face with a touch of primness in it. He saw her eyes move across the powerful symmetry of his muscled torso before returning to his face.

"Mr. Fargo?" she asked.

"In person," he said.

"Shall I wait till you finish dressing?" she asked, and he caught the edge of reproach in her tone.

"You'll have a long wait. I plan on finishing my nap."

"Then I suppose we'd best talk now," she said. "I was afraid you might have already left Tablita. My horse developed a loose shoe on the way here and I was delayed. My name's Abby Tillstrom."

Fargo nodded and took in the rest of her. He saw a slender figure, a tan blouse buttoned to the neck but pleasantly filled out. A black riding skirt hung loosely on almost straight hips, and when she stepped into the room, he noted a round rear filled out the skirt. "What's this about?" Fargo frowned.

"I want to hire you," she said. "I want you to find a cabin for me."

Fargo stared at her incredulously. "A cabin?" he repeated, and she nodded. "Wait, let me guess. A cabin that belonged to Tom Yancey."

Abby Tillstrom's brows lifted in astonishment and her nicely shaped lips fell open. "That's right. How did you know?"

"I've been there before," he said cryptically, and her frown deepened.

"I beg your pardon?"

"It means I know the story."

"But you can't," she insisted.

"But I do, and I'll give you the same answer I gave the others. I've a job waiting to be done. I'm already hired," Fargo said.

"I think you should hear me out. I've come a long way to find you," Abby Tillstrom said stiffly.

"I don't have to hear you out. Tom Yancey was sick or hurt and you helped him. He was so grateful to you that he told you he had a lot of money hidden away and wanted to see that you got some of it. How am I doing so far?" He paused and watched her light-brown eyes continue to stare at him in disbelief.

"Very well, but I don't understand how."

"Then Tom Yancey died. You got a note that told you to go find his cabin. The end," Fargo said. "Tell me I'm wrong."

"No, you're not wrong. But how did you know this?"

"Because two other young ladies, Verna Simpson and Rosalie Hodges, came to me with just about the same story."

"That can't be. It just can't be." Abby Tillstrom frowned.

"Sorry, but it can be. They both came looking to hire me, just as you have. Far as I know, they're still in town," Fargo said.

Abby Tillstrom shook the mantle of shock from her, and anger and determination flooded her voice. "I want to have a talk with them."

"Be my guest." Fargo shrugged. "But one thing, just to satisfy my curiosity. What's your story about helping Tom Yancey?"

"I'm a traveling nurse. Doctors call on me when they need extra help. I was in between jobs, in a small town called Ten Rocks. It was late one night and I was the last customer at the general store when this man rode up. It was plain to see that he was really sick and in terrible pain. He wanted to buy some belladonna or coca leaves, obviously for pain. But the store was out of both. I had a little morphine in my kit at the house where I was staying. I offered to give him some if he could follow me home. He just managed to do so, and I had to help him from his horse when we got there."

"You took him in and gave him the morphine for his pain," Fargo put in, and she nodded.

"He stayed the night, but he needed more in the morning and I gave it to him. He also had chills and I nursed that away after a few days. He said I'd done more for him than any doctor he'd seen," Abby recounted.

"I doubt he'd seen many."

"He admitted that much later," she said. "He stayed for almost two weeks, but there was a limit to what I could do for him. He was a very sick man. I guessed that he had some kind of stomach condition and I thought it quite clear he hadn't long to live without expert treatment, probably surgery. I told him so, and it was then that he told me he was Tom Yancey. He was amused when he learned that I didn't really know about him, having been in this part of the country for only a few months."

"Did he tell you about himself?" Fargo queried.

"Yes, he did, and I was surprised. He didn't seem like a robber and highwayman at all. He seemed very nice, with a quirky sense of humor," Abby Tillstrom recollected.

"He had that," Fargo grunted.

"But I had gotten him feeling much better when he left, though I knew it was only temporary. That's when he told me he'd be thanking me in his own way."

"A variation." Fargo nodded and her light-brown eyes questioned. "Of the stories the other two gals told me," he finished.

Abby spun on her heel and strode from the room. "I have to find them," she said. "But I'll be back."

"Don't bother. I told you I'm hired."

"Money talks."

"Not everybody listens," he called after her, and closed the door. He lay back on the bed wrestling with his own feeling of astonishment. He had seen it as Tom Yancey's last macabre gesture, but maybe the conclusion wasn't completely justified. Maybe. But whatever it was, it was still wrapped in Tom Yancey's odd sense of humor, a gesture that was really more a frustrating riddle than anything else. In any case, it wasn't going to be his problem, Fargo grunted as he let his eyes close again.

This time he napped till it was time to go out and unsaddle the Ovaro. He had just finished dressing when the knock came at the door again. No polite sound this time but a frantic pounding. He strapped on his gun belt and opened the door to see the small figure.

"Fargo, come quick . . . please," Miguel said, his brown eyes wide.

"What is it?"

"At the saloon. Verna is in trouble there. They all are," Miguel said.

"They all are?" Fargo frowned.

"Sí, Verna and the other two, Rosalie and Abby. Please, come before they are hurt."

"All right, all right," Fargo grumbled, and strode from the room with Miguel running a half-pace ahead.

"What the hell are they doing in the saloon?" he asked.

"Just come quickly, please," Miguel pleaded.

Fargo reached the street outside and trotted after Miguel to where the square of yellow light stretched into the dark from the saloon. He slowed when he reached the building, reached out, and pulled the boy back with him as he slipped inside, his back to the wall. He saw the three young women at once. They sat at one of the round tables and some half-dozen men were crowding them as the rest of the customers looked on. Each girl had a heavy beer glass in front of her, two all but emptied, the third half-full.

"You get out of here or we'll throw you out, you hear me?" one of the men shouted, and Fargo saw Rosalie stare back with defiance.

"We've every right to be here. You leave us alone," she snapped.

"The only girls we want in here are the ones that work here," another man said. "And like Jake said, you're making too much goddamn noise."

"We'll be quieter," Fargo heard Abby say placatingly.

"We were arguing. Everybody makes noise in a place like this," Rosalie snapped, no conciliation in her tone whatever.

"You get the hell out of here now," the first man said.

"Stop taking their sass and throw the damn bitches out," someone else shouted. The words served as a trigger and the man called Jake reached for Verna. He had his hands on her when Rosalie crashed her beer glass onto the top of his forehead with a roundhouse swing.

"Owooo, Jesus," he said, and staggered back and fell to one knee as a line of red coursed down his forehead. But the others rushed forward with a roar and Fargo saw two more men join in.

Rosalie kicked another in the leg and he fell back, but other hands seized her and Fargo saw the three girls enveloped, their efforts to fight back now futile. He looked down and saw Miguel's eyes on him.

"Outside," Fargo hissed as he started to back from the saloon.

"You're not going to help them?" Miguel whispered, disappointment and shock in his eyes.

"Not here. Too many people," Fargo said, and pulled the boy with him. Outside, he spun and ran a dozen yards down the street, veered into the deep shadows alongside one of the buildings, and dropped to one knee. Miguel came down alongside him as Fargo watched the men storm from the saloon, yanking the three girls with them, this time with a firm grip on each.

"Goddamn, we'll give you three loudmouth bitches a night to remember," one of the men roared as they dragged their captives with them.

"Bastards," he heard Rosalie snap. Then she cried out in pain as her arm was twisted.

"Shut up," somebody growled, and Fargo drew the Colt, waited silently, and let the group move closer.

"We'll take them to the old shed. We can take our time there," another voice said.

"Yeah, everybody gets a piece of each of them," someone else said. They were within ten yards of where he waited when Fargo raised the Colt and fired. His two shots plowed into the ground an inch from the advancing figures. The men stopped at once as the two little sprays of dirt flew upward. Fargo shifted position and hunkered down behind a big barrel, watching the men peer into the darkness on all sides of them.

"That's enough," he said, and saw the men turn and

peer toward the sound of his voice. "Let them go," he said.

"Like hell," one of the men tossed back.

"That wasn't the right answer," Fargo said and fired again.

The man screamed in pain and fell to one knee as the bullet smashed through his foot. Fargo saw the others start to draw their guns, but then pause, peer into the night, reluctant to do anything to trigger another shot.

"Let them go," Fargo called. "Nobody gets hurt more."

The men waited, exchanged murmurs, and the one with the bleeding foot screamed up at the others. "Let the damn bitches go and help me up," he said. Two of the others released their hold on Rosalie and bent down to help their friend.

"I'm not big on patience. It's always been a fault of mine," Fargo growled.

The others grumbled among themselves, but he saw them release Verna and Abby and begin to back away as they still peered into the black shadows.

"You must be crazy to want these three bitches, mister," one of the men called back.

"Another fault of mine," Fargo said, and stayed in place as the men retreated. He waited till they turned and moved away, the one with the wounded foot hanging on to one of the others for support. When they went back into the saloon, he rose and stepped forward.

Miguel raced past him to clasp his arms around Verna's waist.

"Thanks," Rosalie said.

"Thank Miguel. He came and got me," Fargo said, and saw her put a hand on the boy's head.

"What happened?" Fargo questioned.

"We were arguing in the street and decided to go into the saloon when Abby found us. We sat down, ordered beers, and I guess we got a little noisy," Rosalie said.

"They just didn't want us there," Verna added. "I guess we were making more noise than we realized."

"One came over and told us to leave," Abby Tillstrom said. "He told us we'd no business being there in the first place."

"I told him to leave us alone," Verna said. "Rosalie used some harsher language."

"Then they started to crowd around us," Rosalie said.

"That's where I came in," Fargo said. "You were stupid to go in there in the first place." He saw them shrug, each offering a hint of apology, Rosalie's given with an offhand nod, Verna's a grudging admission, and Abby's cool glance allowing no more than an admission of poor judgment. "What now? You all finished arguing?" Fargo asked.

"No," Verna snapped.

"Damn right not," Rosalie bit out.

"Definitely not," Abby added.

"You going to keep on drawing attention the way manure draws flies?" Fargo prodded.

They exchange frowns. "No, we've had enough of that," Verna said.

"Good luck," he said, turned, and started to walk away.

"Wait," Abby called out. "I still want to talk to you privately."

"Forget it. You have my answer. It goes for all of you." He strode on. He didn't look back, reached the inn, unsaddled the Ovaro, and carried the saddle to his room. He undressed and lay down on the bed. He didn't feel so sorry for them any longer. They had met, argued, and ought to have realized that perhaps they were Tom Yancey's last twisted joke. But desperation adds strength to hope, he realized. So does trust, and they each plainly put a lot of trust in what Yancey had told them.

They were each different, yet none was a naïve schoolgirl. Verna knew the hard side of the world. Rosalie knew the underside. Abby knew the world from her distant disdain, filtering it through an antiseptic primness. Yet each had absorbed Tom Yancey as openly as though they were indeed schoolgirls. The desire to mother and nurse was a powerful force, Fargo realized. How much of that had Yancey deliberately played on? Fargo wondered, and decided further speculation was useless. Otis would surely arrive in the morning, and there'd be more important things to think about then. He closed his eyes and slept almost at once, waking only when the morning sun pushed its way through the window.

He rose, washed and dressed, and hurried outside to halt at what passed for a lobby at the inn. Rosalie, Verna, and Abby were there, plainly waiting for him.

"Good morning," they said in unison, and smiled at him. They looked so pleasant and polite they might have been on a social call.

"No curtsy?" he growled, and saw Abby's lips tighten.

"We don't want to overdo anything," she said.

"You look very chummy," he remarked.

"We made some decisions last night. We took rooms here and stayed up late talking," Verna said.

He eyed the three girls with wariness. "Decisions?" he echoed. "Such as deciding to go back wherever you came from?"

"No. Decisions that will let us combine what we have and what we know," Abby said. "It seems Tom

Yancey did visit each of us, and each of us helped him in our own way. We're convinced of that."

"And we're convinced he wanted to show us his appreciation. We're probably the only three people who ever did anything for him in his whole life," Verna said.

"He's got his own strange ways of showing it, I'd say," Fargo answered.

"That's his way," Rosalie said. "And maybe, in his way, he's protecting us."

"How in hell do you come to that?" Fargo frowned.

"Maybe the only way he can get the money to us is by being secretive about it. Maybe he had to take this way to get to us," Rosalie said. "Any other way would have all kinds of people getting their hands on it."

"You are all bent on seeing things in the best light, aren't you?" Fargo said.

"We think we're right about Tom Yancey," Abby said haughtily. "And we've decided the only way we can find out is by sticking together. I was going to pay you to find the cabin for me. So were Verna and Rosalie. Putting our money together lets us offer you three times as much. We need you."

"You can't understand, can you?" Fargo said. "I gave my word to Otis Frawley. That's an agreement. I'm not breaking it, no matter what you offer."

"A man of principle. That's refreshing," Abby said. "I'm sorry it has to be at our expense."

"It's an unfair world," Fargo said, "Now, good morning, ladies. No, make that good-bye." He walked on and had reached the door of the inn when Abby's voice called after him.

"You can't think that we might be right, can you?" she said accusingly.

"I can think a lot of things, but they all spell trouble," Fargo said. He went on outside and saw Miguel by the hitching post.

"Thank you for saving me, Fargo," the boy said.

"Anytime, Miguel."

"*Adiós,*" Miguel said as Fargo led the Ovaro away. He was halfway through town when he spotted Otis Frawley riding toward him, and he swung onto the horse.

"Sorry I'm late, Fargo. Had to move slowly," Otis said. "I've the herd outside town. Come take a look at them."

Fargo swung onto the Ovaro beside Otis Frawley. An older man, Otis had a round face and a short, stocky frame that reflected the determination that was part of his character. One of the better cattlemen in the Southwest, Otis Frawley believed in careful breeding and he abhorred any kind of waste, whether it was of livestock, food, or men.

As he started to ride alongside Otis, Fargo threw a glance back at the inn. The three young women were outside, Miguel beside them, all staring down the wide street after them. He turned away and refused to let himself feel even a twinge of guilt.

# 3

Fargo's eyes moved over the herd as Otis sat on his horse alongside him. Not a large herd, a little over fifty head, he estimated, all of them whiteface. He let his eyes scan the cattle again, all young heifers, none carrying much fat to burn off. "You said they were special, Otis," he remarked.

"That's right. They're out of a pool of the best breeders in the Southwest. They're going to be sold as foundation stock. Jack Crissel in Tucson is taking the lot," Otis said. "But because of their close breeding, they're not as tough as most stock. They can't go as long, nor can they take the hot sun as long. That's why I want you to break trail through hill country with as much shade as possible."

"That'll mean going out of your way, you know, Otis," Fargo said.

"Fine, as long as I get as much shade as you can find," Otis said. "And I've another reason. There's been a lot of raiding on herds traveling the usual flat routes. I don't want that happening to this herd. There'll only be six of us, four hands and you and me. I kept it to that on purpose. A small crew doesn't draw a lot of attention."

"We'll leave in the morning?" Fargo asked.

Otis nodded. "Tonight, we'll have a good meal and some good whiskey in town. My treat."

"I've never turned down free whiskey." Fargo laughed, and after Otis saw that his men had the herd quiet and in hand, he led the way back through town to the saloon. It had grown dark, but Fargo found himself looking for three shapely figures and was glad he didn't find them. Bourbon and a piece of steer with lots of chili sauce to cover the toughness took care of supper, and old stories took care of the rest of the evening. But finally Otis ran out of stories and they made their way back to the herd. Fargo bedded down under a low-branched dogwood and slept until morning came with a hot sun.

He washed and dressed and saw the others ready to ride. Otis' four hands were plainly experienced men who handled the small herd with quiet ease. Fargo rode forward and waved the herd on. He took the flat road north from town, but quickly turned and headed up to the low hills, which were still mostly sandstone formations with little foliage. He hadn't gone more than fifteen minutes when he spied the figures on the three horses and the one jenny, watching him from a low hill. He swerved and rode up to where they waited.

"We were on our way to meet you when we saw you turn and come up this way," Verna said. "We just wanted to thank you again for the things you did, especially for Miguel and myself."

"No more attempts to buy me?" Fargo commented.

"Wouldn't think of it," Abby said. "We are grateful for past favors, and wanted you to know that." He found her smile more polite than warm, and he glanced at Rosalie.

"Good luck, Fargo," she said. "You're not taking that herd across the plains?"

"No," he said. "And I'd best be getting on. I don't imagine we'll be meeting again."

"You never can tell," Rosalie said.

"It's a small world," Abby put in.

"I'll try to make it bigger," Fargo grunted, let his wave take in everyone, and hurried back to the herd. He skirted the cattle, passed Otis, and moved ahead and up the low hills. He went north, following a passage that led to a line of trees, and continued north to the low hills south of Whitewater Baldy. By the day's end he had the herd moving through hill passes with enough staghorn sumac and bur oak to afford some shade. Just before dark, he found a small ravine where, he saw with glee, a thick cover of needle grass covered the ground. The herd would graze happily on the grass, he knew. He mounted a hill and waved them forward.

He dismounted, lay the saddle on the ground, and sat up at the edge of the small ravine when Otis arrived with the herd. The heifers immediately set upon the tasty needle grass and Otis nodded happily. "Probably the only ravine like it up here," Otis said.

"Probably," Fargo agreed.

"And you found it. But that's why I hired you." Otis laughed and made off to find a spot to bed down.

Fargo took his bedroll and settled down to sleep on a sweet cushion of good bourbon, and the world drifted away. The night was dark, and deep into the hanging hours before the dawn, he snapped awake, the shots reverberating in the ravine like thunderclaps. He sat up as two more shots exploded, and he'd just pulled on his trousers and his gun belt when he had to dive sideways as a half-dozen wildly charging, thousand-pound bodies hurtled toward him. He landed in a patch of dry brush and felt the ends stab into his naked torso. He rolled and pushed to his feet to see that the night had become alive with the huge dark forms stampeding in every direction.

Some raced to the far end of the small ravine, he saw, while others charged up the side passages. They'd been so startled that they didn't stampede as a herd but ran in different directions. Fargo drew his Colt and began to run alongside another half-dozen racing forms. He fired over their backs, and they swerved but raced up another passage without slowing even a fraction. Three thundering forms appeared, driving straight at him, and again he flung himself sideways to avoid being trampled. He regained his feet to see the cattle disappearing up the sides of the ravine.

He heard Otis shouting commands, but most of the herd was already out of sight, the four cowhands chasing sounds more than bodies. They were already scattering in the blackness of the hills, he knew, running alone or in small groups. They'd run until they were exhausted and then continue wandering aimlessly through the labyrinth of hill passages. They'd be so skittish now that they'd take off in a run again at any unexpected sound.

Fargo walked back to his bedroll, sank down on the saddle where it lay on the ground, and holstered the Colt. Dawn peered over the hills when two of the cowhands returned with three heifers, and he saw Otis halt before them.

"They're all over the damn hills," one of the men said. "They scattered so wide I figure it'll take a month to find them, and another three weeks to bring them in."

"We'll have to do it when daylight comes," Otis said. "No matter how long it takes. We'll chase down the ones the cougars and wolves don't get, or those that don't kill themselves in panic, and bring them back to the ranch." He turned to where Fargo listened, resignation and bitterness in his round face. "That's all I can do now. They're too valuable to just forget about. But there won't be a drive to Tucson now, Fargo, not till next season. I'll pay your price. It's not your fault," he said.

"It's not yours, either, Otis. There'll be no paying," Fargo said, and put one hand on Otis' shoulder.

"Appreciate that, Fargo," the man muttered.

"What the hell happened? I heard shots," Fargo said.

"Probably some goddamn night hunters in the hills," Otis said. "Too damn close, though. And it's plain they didn't look around any. I hope they got themselves stomped into the ground." He stalked off still muttering, and Fargo returned to his bedroll and lay down, unhappy for Otis. He was a good man who didn't deserve bad breaks. But then goodness was an uncertain shield in this world, he had learned that long ago. Fargo was still thinking about what had happened. Why were night hunters in these low hills? He frowned in disapproval. They could only have been after small game, a few night prowlers, bobcat, possum, and raccoon. Damn shame, he murmured, and closed his eyes to catch another hour of sleep until the sun came up full over the hills.

He woke again, then said his good-bye to Otis. The four hands rode away on the start of their search and Fargo saddled the Ovaro and slowly wandered through the hills. He let himself enjoy the rust red of the sandstone formations, the slow, wheeling flight of a Swainson's hawk, and halted to admire the brilliant scarlet blossoms of a thorny ocotillo shrub. He followed a narrow passage downward between tall rocks and then reined to a sudden halt, his brows lifting in surprise. The three horses and the mule were standing quietly in a flat area alongside a crusted rock, and as he stared, Rosalie stepped into view from behind the rock. Abby appeared next, then Verna, Miguel beside her. The three young women looked at him with quiet surprise as he rode over to them.

"What are you doing up here?" Fargo frowned.

"Exploring, looking," Rosalie said. "We're trying to find a cabin, remember?"

"Still joining forces, are you?" Fargo said.

"That's right," Verna said.

"The truth is, we were looking for you," Rosalie said. "Seeing as how you can help us now."

Fargo felt a sudden seed stir inside him, not formed yet but nonetheless very much there. "How'd you know that?" he questioned sharply.

"We met one of the cowhands searching through the hills. He told us what had happened," Verna said. "No more herd, no more need for you to break trail."

Fargo felt the seed inside himself beginning to grow. "Sort of a convenient coincidence, isn't it?" he remarked.

"The world's full of coincidences," Rosalie said.

Fargo swung from the Ovaro and strode to the gray mare. He lifted the horse's left forefoot and right hindfoot, peered at each hoof, and went on to Rosalie's horse, where he did the same. When he lifted the right foreleg of Abby's horse, he pulled a handful of small stalks from the edge of the shoe. "Needle grass," he snapped, "It's on the other hooves, too, and the only needle grass around here is in that ravine."

Rosalie summoned a brazen stare while Verna shrugged and Abby held on to an innocent expression. "Coincidence, my ass," Fargo barked. "You little bitches! You stampeded that herd. No damn night hunters. You three." He burned angry glares at each and caught the furtive glances Verna exchanged with

Rosalie. "I ought to drag you back to Otis and let him decide what to do with you," Fargo said as the amazement curled inside him.

"You can't prove that," Rosalie tossed back.

"We could have ridden through the ravine this morning," Abby said.

"Nobody went through the ravine this morning, and you know it," Fargo said.

"We don't know anything of the sort," Verna said as he continued to stare at them in amazement. They were sticking together and to their story. But then, they couldn't do less. He had underestimated them, he realized as the amazement clung to him. "You really can't prove anything," Verna said. "Taking us to Otis Frawley won't help anybody or anything."

"Why do you think that?" he asked.

"It won't bring his herd back, will it? It won't get you the money you're out, and it won't help us any," she said.

"Convenient logic to go with convenient coincidence?" he tossed back.

"It still holds," Verna said.

He swore inwardly, unwilling to concede the point, and turned away to stare narrow-eyed out into the distant hills. They were so different from one another, Rosalie was buxom worldly brashness, Verna slender quiet perseverance, and Abby was coolly cerebral purposeness. Yet Tom Yancey had reached each of them, convinced each he had chosen her for his gratitude. Or perhaps he had only managed to touch a need, a desperate want to believe in someone. Fargo grunted, snapped off thoughts, and turned back to the three girls. Despite his anger, Verna's logic still held, self-serving as it was.

"There's only one way I'll help you," he said. "You've cost Otis a heap of money. If this whole thing isn't just

Tom Yancey's last joke, he's got to have a lot of loot hidden away. We find it, and you promise you'll pay Otis what you cost him."

"All right, but we're still not admitting anything," Abby said, and Rosalie and Verna nodded agreement.

"Settled," Fargo said, and he fastened his eyes on Miguel. "And we leave Miguel at the first town."

"No," Miguel cried out.

"Miguel goes with me," Verna protested. "He won't be any trouble."

"You'll all be trouble," Fargo barked. "You'll be going through hard, dangerous country, no place for any of you."

"You're being paid to take us. The rest is our decision and our risk," Abby said, the cool reproach in her voice again.

"Only it never works out that way," Fargo grunted. "Three foolish girls and a little boy. I must be out of my mind. Mount up."

He set off down hill and moved westward through the rock formations. He held a slow pace and glanced back at the others as they followed. Rosalie came first, her deep breasts swaying and bouncing as the horse took the difficult footing. Verna's tight, slender body moved well with her horse, while Abby rode with stiff-backed control that would soon make her damn tired, he knew.

When he halted at a trickle of a mountain stream, the midday sun was blazing. Rosalie's shirt, wet with perspiration, clung to the deep curves of her breasts and outlined large nipples. Verna had her blouse hung out loose at the bottom, the fabric only touching her breasts in quick, tantalizing moments. Abby's face was flushed with heat, and spots of perspiration shone on the back of her blouse, which she kept buttoned up to the neck.

She knelt beside him and put her wrists into the thin stream, and he saw her close her eyes in relief. "You keep your sleeves down and your blouse all buttoned up and you'll get yourself heatstroke," he told her.

She opened her eyes and fastened him with a cool stare. "Clothing can be a protection against the heat. The Arabs wear robes that cover them from head to foot in the heat of the desert," she said.

"Do they, now?" he said.

"Yes. I'm afraid you'll have to be content with Rosalie and Verna," she said stiffly.

"Whatever you say, honey." Fargo smiled and pushed to his feet. "Let's ride."

He climbed into the saddle and set out again, casting a glance at Miguel on the jenny. Both were handling the dry, burning heat with ease. Fargo moved downward again, threading a maze of passages where the heat radiated from the sunbaked rocks in waves. He glanced back at the girls. Rosalie was still perspiring profusely, her blouse thoroughly wet and clinging to her like a wet leaf. She carried ten, maybe fifteen pounds of extra weight, he murmured inwardly. Verna's loose shirttails kept her the coolest of the lot, and he saw Abby's face had become very flushed.

He had almost reached the bottom of the last passage when he heard Rosalie cry out. He spun in the saddle and saw that she was hanging on to Abby's limp, unconscious form with one arm to keep her from falling from her horse.

Fargo turned the Ovaro and hurried back, and he saw Verna had come up to help. "Ease her to the ground," he said.

"She just fainted. I was riding alongside her," Rosalie said.

"Passed out from the heat," Fargo said as he dropped down beside Abby. He yanked the high-buttoned blouse half-open and rubbed water from his canteen along her prominent collarbones and halfway down over small-ish breasts, then he bathed her neck and face. "Loosen her skirt," he ordered, and Rosalie pulled open the strings. He put his hat over Abby's head and rubbed more water over her face, neck, and collarbones, her skin burning under his touch. He felt her begin to cool with another application of water, and she finally groaned, stirred, and opened her eyes. He raised her head and let her take in small sips of water.

When she was able to sit up, he leaned back and she blinked at him. Her hand came up, touched her wet collarbones and automatically started to pull her blouse closed.

Fargo slapped her hand away roughly and saw pro-test form in her eyes. "You want to stay modest or stay alive?" he growled, and she let her hand fall to her side. "You wear my hat, roll up your sleeves, and keep those damn buttons open," he said, and rose and helped her to her feet. "When we reach Carmela, you're all going to buy hats—wide-brimmed straw ones if possible," he said, and watched Abby pull herself into the saddle, most of her face covered by his hat.

"Thank you," she murmured as Verna and Rosalie returned to their horses. "I don't understand how the Arabs do it," she said.

"Those robes are loose so they have a layer of air protecting their bodies," he said. "You'll be all right now. The sun's not bearing down on us any longer. It'll be dark in another hour or so, and we ought to be at Carmela by then."

"Why are we going there?" Verna asked.

"Because I'm not riding these hills till I'm gray. I need a lead, maybe something more about Yancey. There's a sheriff in Carmela. Maybe he can tell me something. There's also an inn. You can get a good night's sleep and we'll take on fresh water tomorrow," Fargo said, and set a slow pace the rest of the way.

Dusk fell as they reached the town, which was filled with flat-roofed, whitewashed buildings. It had a more Mexican look to it than most towns near the border. Fargo halted at a square, stucco building that advertised BED AND BOARD. "Get me a room and do the same for yourselves," he said. "I'll be along later."

He went off in a trot until he found the sheriff's office, a narrow room with a single window. A sign hung in the door: BE BACK TOMORROW. Fargo sighed. Law and order were not a priority business in Carmela. He turned the pinto and rode back to the inn, where he saw Miguel seated outside, a heavy key in his hand.

"Room Two, Fargo," the boy said, and handed him the key.

"Take the saddle off the jenny," Fargo told him as he unsaddled the Ovaro. "Get her some oats at the general store in the morning."

"Sí," Miguel said. "Shall I give your horse a rubdown?"

"Give yourself a rubdown and get some sleep." Fargo smiled. "There'll be lots of hard riding ahead." Miguel nodded happily. It was all just another adventure to him, death and danger were only words. Perhaps he was right, Fargo thought.

The Trailsman walked to his room and found a single bed, a lamp, and a tin bucket of water. A narrow window opened at the top allowed a warm breeze of night air to enter. He felt a stab of hunger and went outside, walked the main street, and found a cantina open. He had just finished a bowl of chili and was starting to leave when Verna, Rosalie, and Abby appeared, Miguel in tow.

They had freshened up and were chatting happily. Even Abby seemed fully restored. But she had his hat on, her blouse was modestly unbuttoned, and the sleeves were rolled up, he noted with satisfaction.

"You find the sheriff?" Verna asked.

"He'll be back tomorrow. I'll talk to him while you get your hats," Fargo said. "The chili's good."

"See you in the morning," Verna said, and Fargo hurried back to the inn, undressed, and stretched out on the bed. He slept quickly until he was wakened by a soft rapping at the door. He turned the lamp on low, pulled on trousers, and opened the door to see Rosalie standing there in a loose, long pink nightgown.

"Came to talk to you," she murmured, and slipped into the room.

"After the others are asleep," he said, a faint smile touching his lips. She half-shrugged, her deep breasts lifting against the nightgown, and he glimpsed large dark circles in the center of each through the thin material. "Am I right in thinking the alliance isn't all that strong?" he remarked blandly.

"We decided we'd do best by working together. Nobody said we were bosom buddies," she returned.

"Nice choice of words," Fargo remarked, and she made a face at him. "You going to apply that phrase to us?" He smiled.

"Something like that," Rosalie said. "I don't know what Verna or Abby will be like when we actually find the money—"

"If you find it," Fargo interrupted.

"Whatever," she said impatiently. "They might be fair or they might go wild. We might stick together, or everything could fall apart. I want to be able to count on you." She stepped forward and lifted her arms to encircle his neck. "I want to thank you in advance," she murmured.

"It wouldn't be gentlemanly to refuse," Fargo murmured.

"No, it wouldn't be," Rosalie said, and her full lips were on his, pressing hard. He felt the heat of her body through the thin fabric. His hands found the shoulders of the nightgown, pushed, and the garment came free and slid to the floor. He lowered Rosalie to the bed as he took in the deep breasts, just avoiding flabbiness, each tipped by a brownish nipple and a brown-pink areola. A wide spring of ribs gave her an added fullness, and he saw a round belly and, below it, a large, thick patch that fringed onto full thighs as though it were trying to grow larger. Her legs were full, again with ten pounds too much weight on them, but she was still young enough to carry it.

Her hand behind his neck pulled his mouth down to her. She kissed him hungrily, then paused as he shed trousers, and he saw the small wild light glisten in her light-blue eyes.

He pressed himself half over her, and she made a groaning sound as her mouth held his, her tongue reaching out, moving from side to side. He closed a hand around one deep breast, pushed up to the brown tip, ran his finger back and forth over its firmness, and Rosalie gave a half-groan, half-sigh as her body turned toward him. He drew himself over her round, full figure and felt her skin suddenly damp. When he pressed his throbbing maleness against her, she groaned again, a deep sound, and her lips worked, beckoned, closed around his mouth as he came to her. He let his firmness rub through the black patch and felt the very round Venus mound below.

"Oh, Jesus," Rosalie gasped out, and her full thighs fell open at once. He rested his tip almost against the top of the quivering portal and brought his mouth to one deep breast and pulled, aware that gentleness was not for Rosalie as her hands became fists that pounded against his back.

"Jesus, take me, now, now," Rosalie murmured, thrusting her full hips upward. He felt the roundness of her belly slap against his flat, muscled abdomen. Calculation had quickly turned to wanting with Rosalie, and her eyes were afire and her full thighs lifted to crush against his legs. He lowered his body, found her waiting and eager portal, and slid forward. "Oh, oh, aaaaah, ah, Jesus," Rosalie groaned, and thrust upward to meet him, and as her thighs clasped against his body, she began to utter guttural little groans, each one deeper and stronger than the one before, until suddenly there was but one long, growling groan.

His mouth took as much as it could of one deep breast as it jiggled and fell sideways, and finally he felt her arms tighten around his back, her groan becoming a sudden half-whispered growl. "Aaaagghhhh . . ." Rosalie pressed her full-fleshed body hard against him, jiggled against his muscled hardness as her hips continued to push upward with quick thrusts. He let himself explode with her, immersed totally in her round, soft enveloping ecstasy.

Finally, with a long sigh, she fell back and he licked tiny beads of perspiration from the brown-pink nipples. "Oh, God, that was special . . . oh, God," she whispered.

"Even without a reason?" he slid at her.

"Even without a reason," she murmured. She lay still, drew in deep breaths, and her heavy breasts rose and fell with each until finally she pushed herself up on one elbow. "But there's something else," she said. "Another reason." He felt his brows lift. She turned on her stomach, her full rear end rising into the air, and she put her finger on her right buttock, near her hip where she could twist her head to see. He stared at a small tattoo and brought his eyes to hers. "Tom Yancey did that," she said, and he frowned back.

"Seems you gave your all to Yancey, too," he said.

"No. He was too sick to do anything. But he had this tattoo needle and kit in his saddlebag. He said he liked to do tattoos, and this one would be important in finding the money he'd hidden."

"How?" Fargo frowned, and she shrugged, her full rear shaking with the motion.

"It has to mean something, like a clue," Rosalie said.

Fargo peered at the tattoo again and saw a narrow pyramid without a baseline, but along the bottom of the pyramid there were four small squares. It seemed absolutely meaningless, and again Fargo wondered about Tom Yancey's bizarre sense of humor. "I guess we'll just have to wait and see if it makes any sense in time," he said, and rubbed his hand across the smooth, very full rear.

Rosalie turned over and reached for the nightgown. "It will. I'm sure of it," she said, pulled the garment on, and rose to her feet as he went to the door with her.

"Do the wrong thing and tonight won't count a damn," he warned her, and she nodded and waved at him as she slipped from the room. But she was pleased with herself. It had been in her eyes. She'd come for extra insurance and enjoyed every minute of it. But she'd received less than she thought. He'd play no favorites. He returned to the bed and slept at once till morning dawned.

After drinking a cup of strong coffee he strolled down the street and found the sheriff in his office, a thin man with a quiet mien.

"Tom Yancey?" he echoed at Fargo's question. "The man you want to see is in Horse Bend, about twenty miles north. He's retired now, but when he was sheriff, he chased Yancey so often and so long that he knows him like a brother. He's the man who can tell you about Tom Yancey. His name's Gil Breaker."

"Much obliged. I'll go visit him," Fargo said, and returned to the inn, where he waited for the three girls. They finally appeared, each sporting a straw hat, and Abby handed him back his Stetson. "Saddle up. We've a visit to make," he said, and finally rode from the town a little before noon. He had ridden perhaps an hour when he saw the dark, almost black clouds build in the sky, warning of a powerful thunderstorm. His eyes swept the rocks and he spied a deep ledge with an overhang. He headed up the passage toward it.

The climb grew steep, and he slowed to let the girls catch up. Finally they drew onto a wide, flat ledge of rock. A vivid flash of lightning split the sky, quickly followed by a tremendous thunderclap. Fargo led the way under the overhang and saw it was deep enough to let everyone move to the back. He dismounted, tethered the Ovaro to a jagged edge of rock, and helped Verna secure her gray.

The rain came, driven by high winds and accompanied by the violent lightning and fierce thunder of a tremendous storm. "Move among the horses, pat them, keep them calm," he ordered, and Miguel was quickest to obey.

The hills seemed to become a giant cannon that fired ceaselessly. Fargo helped keep the horses calm, no small task in the reverberating crescendo of sound. But finally the terrible roar began to fade into a low rumble, and then it vanished as the storm passed on. The driving rain stopped, and Fargo walked to the edge of the ledge and watched the muddy water course down the rock passages, swift-moving streams of small pebbles and sandstone silt, too treacherous for the horses to negotiate. "We'll have to wait until it runs off, probably another two hours," he said to the others. "Sit down, relax, take a nap."

He lowered himself against the rocks near the edge of the ledge and watched the others settle down. Miguel came and sat beside him, and Fargo smiled inwardly at the small gesture of friendship.

The sky began to turn gray in the late afternoon when he decided the passages were clear enough to negotiate without danger, and he led the way downward, silently swearing at the uncooperative weather. Dusk began to sweep the land when he reached Horse Bend, and he halted at the general store and inquired about Gil Breaker. "You'll find him at the sheriff's office," the storekeeper said. "He's retired, but he's never really accepted that, so he helps out and stays close to the job. He enjoys being on the edge."

"Thanks," Fargo said, and the three young women followed him as he rode on. He paused before a weathered frame building with a sign outside and nodded to Verna. "Same as last night. Get me a room. I'll be along later," he said, and hurried on. He entered the sheriff's office, and a gray-haired man with a ruddy face lounged in a straight-backed chair. "Looking for Gil Breaker," Fargo said.

"You found him," the man answered.

"Name's Fargo . . . Skye Fargo."

"The Trailsman?" Gil Breaker asked, and Fargo nodded. "Glad to meet up with you. Heard about you often enough. What brings you to Horse Bend?"

"Need some information about Tom Yancey," Fargo said. "I've heard a lot of stories about his strange ways. They're all true, I take it."

"I'm sure they are. It'd be hard to make up some of the things Tom Yancey did," the man said, and Fargo let him fall into a half-dozen stories.

"Then he really had the crazy sense of humor everyone talks about," Fargo said.

"He did, and he was slick and smart and clever as well. I decided he robbed for the plain fun of it. Most bandits are mean and nervous when they pull off their jobs, but Tom Yancey was never like that. It all seemed like a grand game to him. That's why he did all the strange things he did. The average bandit takes his victims' guns, sometimes their horses, to keep them from chasing after him. One time Tom Yancey got the drop on a posse and made them strip down naked as jaybirds. He took off with their clothes and left them their guns and horses. He got away clean because nobody wanted to go chasing him around stark-naked."

"You ever hear about his tattooing anybody?" Fargo questioned.

"Hell, yes. Tattooing was a hobby of his. Another of his foolish quirks," Breaker said. "Once he held up a stage, men and women on it, took their guns, and then made them stand still while he tattooed each one on the arm."

"What'd he put on them?" Fargo asked.

"Robbed by Tom Yancey," Gil Breaker roared, and Fargo thought quietly to himself for a long moment. In its own strange way, everything Verna, Rosalie, and Abby had said was holding together. But it could still all be no more than Tom Yancey's last joke, and Fargo voiced the question he'd saved for last.

"He was a sick man for some while before he died in that doc's office," Fargo said. "Yet while a sick and dying man, he managed to pull off a last job, I heard, the robbery of a silver-mine payroll."

"He did, and he got away with all of it," the retired sheriff said. "He was one of a kind."

"Where'd he pull this last robbery?"

"In the low land west of Magdalena, on a road bordered by hackberry on both sides," Breaker said, and sat back in the chair. "Now, do you mind telling me why you have all this interest in Tom Yancey?"

"Three young ladies think he left them all the loot nobody ever found. He did a damn good job of convincing them of it. But he gave them nothing but talk, vague hints, and wild clues. They hired me to help them," Fargo said. It was the truth, and there was no need to go into Yancey's talk about a cabin. "You think he was having a last joke?"

"Wouldn't put it past him. Wouldn't put it past him to be telling them something important, either," the man said. "Guess I'm not being real helpful."

"You have been, Gil," Fargo said. "You've filled in a picture of Yancey. That's plenty. I'm beholden to you."

"Anytime," the man said, offered a hearty handshake, and Fargo hurried into the night. Gil Breaker had done more than fill in a picture. He had given a starting place, a thread to go on, slender as it was. Fargo rode back to the inn, where a heavyset woman behind the desk handed him a key.

"Last room end of the hall," she said, and Fargo strode down the dimly lighted corridor and entered the room. It was much like all rooms in small-town inns: the lone bed, the lamp, and the water basin. He left the door open when he went back outside and unsaddled the Ovaro, and he was carrying the saddle in when the three figures stepped from their rooms, Verna first, then Rosalie and Abby. "What did you find out?" Verna asked.

"Maybe something, maybe nothing. We'll talk in the morning," Fargo said, and strode on to his room. He set the saddle in a corner, undressed, and stretched out across the bed. He wanted to feel hopeful and encouraged, but he could feel only uneasiness. He'd never taken part in something so real that seemed so unreal, and once again he had Tom Yancey to thank for that. He closed his eyes, stopped thinking, and let himself sleep.

He was wakened a few hours later and found himself with a half-smile as he pulled on his trousers. Midnight visitors were getting to be a habit, and he felt a moment of surprise when he opened the door and didn't find Rosalie's ample figure.

"I had to come see you," Verna said, a blue bathrobe wrapped tightly around her tall, slender figure.

"Alone, at this hour, when everyone else is asleep," Fargo said, using words hardly different from those he'd used the night before.

"That's right," Verna said, and he closed the door as her eyes moved across his muscled torso. "I've things to say."

Fargo sank down on the edge of the bed. "Say them."

"You helped Miguel because you thought it right. Then you helped me. I know you do things because you want to, not just because you're being paid to. And I feel closer to you than Rosalie or Abby," she said. "I want to stay that way, closer."

"So far you're doing fine," Fargo allowed.

"If we find that cabin and the money, I don't know what the others will do, and I've Miguel to think about. Money has a way of turning people inside out. I want to be sure that doesn't happen. I want to know you'll be there to take care of Miguel and me if it comes to that."

Fargo nodded. The words were different, but the melody was pretty much the same. Verna's little speech was a variation of Rosalie's. "Anything more?" he asked.

"Not now. I said I felt closer to you, I've been around long enough to know that there's saying and there's proving," she said, and he saw her hands suddenly pull at the belt of the robe. The garment fell open and she shrugged her body, shoulders twisting, and the robe fell to the floor. She wore nothing under it, and he let his eyes enjoy her tall, slender loveliness.

She had modest breasts with deep-red tips on small pink circles, breasts that curved at the cups with a nice line, firm and tight, no dip or sag to them, and below, a small waist that gave her an hourglass figure. Fargo then took in her flat abdomen, almost flat belly, nicely rounded hips, and a neat black nap that ended at the top of long, tapered legs, on the thin edge yet shapely enough.

She stepped forward, arms sliding around his neck, and with a sudden motion he pulled at her and spun her onto the bed on her back. His eyes stayed on her as he shed his trousers. He saw no fear in her face. Instead, he saw a faint flush of excitement touch her face, and her glance went down to him again, appreciation in her eyes as she saw him already burgeoning, his body replying to hers. Her mouth was open and waiting when he pressed his lips to it, and her tongue darted, slid back and forth, deliciously wet and exciting. Her brown hair fell in a small cascade against the pillow, and he saw the smile slide across her face.

"Oh, oh, yes," Verna murmured as his face pressed down against the modest breasts, his lips moving from one deep red nipple to the other, circling, exciting each tip to grow firm. His hand moved down over her with slow caresses and Verna's legs moved together in unison, then fell apart, came back together again.

"Yes, oh, yes . . . good, nice, so nice," she murmured as her own hands moved up and down his body pressing, soothing, digging in harder as she responded to his touch. "Yes, yes," Verna murmured again as his hand moved down over her slender body, pushed through the neat nap, and felt the swollen mound under it. He felt Verna press herself against him, her slender legs straightening, lifting, then straightening again and suddenly wrapping themselves around his powerful thighs. She thrust her flat belly against his throbbing maleness, rubbing back and forth as she uttered low moans of delight. No heaving, edge-of-crudeness passion for Verna, none of Rosalie's unvarnished earthiness, but a driving passion of her own, wanting with an edge to it, ecstasy as determined as the thrust of her chin.

"Take me, Fargo, take me, take me . . . God, now, now," Verna whispered urgently, and he felt the taut slenderness of her quivering under him. He let his hand explore her, and she half-screamed as he caressed the dark wetness of her. She pulled his mouth down, thrust her breast into it, and cried out again as he enveloped her in warm moistness. Her slender figure quivered, urged, demanded, and he could no longer hold back his own burning. He came to her, a hard, deep thrust, its own release. Verna gasped and her slender legs rose, clasped themselves around the small of his back, and she bucked with him, finding the rhythm at once, driving with him, clinging, pushing, gasping, bodies locked, suddenly no longer man and woman but flesh on flesh, ecstasy on ecstasy, all one, all joined together in pleasure beyond the senses.

He felt her close around him, her body shaking with miniature convulsions, and she was half-screaming into his ear, arms locked around his neck. "Now, now . . . oh, sweet coming . . . oh, oh, oooooh," Verna cried, and she screamed as she felt his eruption joining hers.

He heard her half-whimpered gasps as the ecstasy vanished too soon, small sounds of despair pushed into his chest, and finally she fell away from him. He lay with her, the comfort of passion still holding them together, and finally he rolled to lay beside her. He enjoyed the long, slender beauty of her, a woman's figure that echoed a girl's body.

She pulled her eyes open finally and reached up to caress his cheek with one hand.

"What if there is no money? You going to be sorry you came visiting?" he asked.

"No, not ever," Verna said. "I can call it thanking you for helping Miguel and me. Or I can call it just wonderful."

"Your choice," he said, and his eyes enjoyed watching her slender body move as she sat up on one elbow, her breast touching his chest.

"There's one thing more, something Tom Yancey did," she said as she flipped onto her stomach and turned up her tight, firm little rear. He saw the tattoo mark on her right buttock at once, in the same place Rosalie's had been, where she could see it by twisting her head around.

"That all he did?" Fargo asked. He decided to stay with the same questions he had asked Rosalie and see if he got different answers.

"That's all he could do," Verna said. "He told me it'd help me find where he'd hidden the money." Fargo studied the tattoo and saw it was exactly the same as Rosalie's, the narrow pyramid without a bottom line and beneath the two sides of the pyramid, the four small squares. Verna let him examine it and suddenly turned on her side, a furrow creasing her brow. "You don't seem very surprised," she slid at him.

"I don't surprise easily," he said quickly, but the furrow became a frown.

"I show you a tattoo Tom Yancey did on my ass and you don't surprise easily?" she said, her voice tightening. "Maybe that's because you've seen it before?" He said nothing as he wondered what he ought to answer. But Verna had seized the thought and ran with it as she swung around, her legs touching the floor. "Was Rosalie here? Did she have one, too?" Verna asked. "Did she come here to try to butter up to you?"

"Is that wrong? Unfair?" he asked mildly, and saw her start to snap out an answer and pull her lips closed as his question reached her.

"My coming here is different. We're closer. I told you that," she said.

"So you did," he agreed, and saw she knew her answer was flimsy as her lips tightened. "Did she really have a tattoo?" Verna asked him.

"Why don't you ask her?" he said.

Verna frowned. "I'm sure we'll find out what it means as soon as we find his cabin."

"I'm glad you're sure," Fargo grunted, and watched the tight, slender shape disappear inside the blue bathrobe. He rose and went to the door with her.

She leaned against him for a moment. "I'm still glad I came," she murmured.

"Me, too," he said. "Now get some sleep. We've a lot of riding, come morning."

She slipped from the room and Fargo returned to the bed. It was still bizarre, still unreal, but unreality had its rewards, and he smiled as he went to sleep.

# 4

When morning came, Fargo took the time to let everyone breakfast on hot biscuits and coffee in town. He stocked up on beef jerky and led the way out of Horse Bend with the sun at mid-morning. He headed northwest, staying on flat land as much as possible, but the terrain didn't allow that luxury for long as it became craggy and filled with sandstone hills.

"Where are we going?" Verna asked when he paused to let the horses rest in the shade of a conelike hillock.

"Alegrosa Mountain," Fargo said.

"Why?" Rosalie queried.

"Something Gil Breaker said," Fargo answered. "I'll tell you more when we get there. Let's ride." He set off at a faster pace and halted more frequently for short rests. By midafternoon they had ridden west past Magdalena until he drew to a halt at a road that lay on the edge of the foothills of Alegrosa Mountain, a road bordered on each side by a growth of hackberry. "This is where Tom Yancey pulled his last job, the robbery of a silver-mine payroll," Fargo said. "He was a sick and dying man then. He probably did it as a last laugh, or to prove something to himself."

"Probably," Verna agreed. "But how does that help us?"

"We know he was a sick man. He wouldn't be riding for days. He probably couldn't. So, he'd do his last job close to home," Fargo said, and his eyes went to the hills that climbed high to become Alegrosa Mountain. "I'd guess that his cabin is somewhere up in the mountain."

He heard all three girls draw in sharp breaths of instant excitement. It faded quickly as they turned their eyes up to the mountain land, rugged and covered with red cedar, gambel oak, and thick growths of piñon pine.

"It'll still be like looking for a needle in a haystack," Rosalie muttered.

"Maybe not," Fargo said. "We'll start at the bottom and move slowly, but not today. There's not enough light left. I'll find us a place to bed down." He moved forward, crossed the road and threaded his way through the hackberry and into the low hills. He found a spot in a small hollow surrounded by red cedar, and Rosalie dismounted quickly and stretched out on a bed of fern moss, clearly exhausted from the day's hard ride. Verna sat down near her with a frown, and Fargo gave Miguel a handful of the beef jerky strips to pass around.

"Where are you going?" Abby asked as he took his bedroll down and left his saddle on the ground beside the pinto.

"Up there," he said, and gestured beyond the cedars at the back of the hollow. "You get to sleep as soon as you've eaten." He walked away into the cedar as the twilight filtered down, and found a place for himself before night fell, not more than a hundred yards above the hollow. He lay down, still dressed, and took in a deep breath of the sweet smell of red cedar.

He'd relaxed for only a half-hour when he heard the sound, footsteps tentatively moving through the trees.

He waited, then finally saw the small form come into sight. "Over here," he called, and the form changed direction, hurried forward, and took on definite shape, light-brown hair, a thin body and smallish breasts touching the tan blouse. He felt surprise and realized he had somehow held Abby as being unlike Verna and Rosalie.

"The others can't be asleep yet," he said.

"No, but they're having an argument," Abby said as she halted in front of him.

"That bothered you," he said, and she nodded.

"Their argument did," Abby answered. "It was about their tattoos. Verna started it."

"Figures," he commented. "Why'd that bother you so?"

"Because I have one too," Abby said, and now he really felt the surprise push at him.

"I'll be damned. All that properness disappeared with Tom Yancey, did it?" he said.

"No, it most certainly did not," she sniffed. "But he said that the tattoo would be important in the future. He was really so nice and seemed so sincere that I let him do it, on the back of my knee."

She carefully pulled her skirt up to her knee and he saw a smooth-skinned leg, a little on the thin side, but the calf had a nice curve to it. "I decided nobody would be likely to see it there," Abby said as she turned so he could see the back of her knee. He studied the tattoo, again exactly the same one as on Verna and Rosalie, and Abby quickly let the skirt drop back in place. "Do you make anything of it?" she asked.

"No more than I did the other two. They're all the same."

"The same?" Abby echoed.

"The only difference is the place," he said.

She wanted to ask, the question in her eyes, but she

turned away from it. "What does it mean?" she asked instead.

"I don't know," he said honestly.

"You still think it's all part of Tom Yancey's last joke."

"Could damn well be," Fargo said.

"No, it's not. It's his way, his weird way of doing things, but it means something more than a last joke. If he'd done it to only one of us, I might agree. But not all three of us. It's too much."

"Maybe you're right. Damned if I can decide," Fargo said. "Let's see what the cabin brings, if we can find it."

She nodded and started to turn away.

"You could stay the night," he said.

She returned a coolly disdainful glance. "Is that what Rosalie and Verna did when they showed you their tattoos?"

"Now, you know it wouldn't be gentlemanly to answer that."

"You just did," she tossed back smugly, and walked on.

He watched her disappear into the trees and sank down on the bedroll. "Smartass," he grumbled, undressed, and stretched out. For a few moments he'd thought that he hadn't read Abby right, but he had—a thing of small satisfaction, he admitted. He closed his eyes and let sleep come quickly.

Fargo woke with the new day as it spread over the hills. He washed, dressed, and went down to where the girls waited. Miguel was already atop the jenny. Verna shot him a tight-lipped glance and he saw Rosalie's round face in a glower. Abby met his glance with cool silence.

"You all spend the night arguing or comparing?" he queried.

74

"Dammit, Fargo, we don't know anything anymore. We believed in what he said to each of us," Rosalie bit out.

"And in what he did," Fargo put in mildly.

"Yes, we believed, and now we wonder if maybe he was just playing games with us," she went on. "We just don't know now."

"Well, I know one thing: I haven't come all this way to turn around. I'm going to see if I can find a cabin. I expect you'll come along?" Fargo said.

"Yes, of course," Abby said, and the others sniffed agreement.

The Trailsman moved on into the hills, made his way deeper and higher into the foothills where Alegrosa Mountain peered down on the thick cover of spruce, red cedar, and cottonwoods that formed a green blanket over the harshness of rock passages. He had climbed carefully, wandered with seeming aimlessness, but his lake-blue eyes ceaselessly swept the ground and the trees on all sides. Miguel left the others to ride beside him, and Fargo muttered inwardly at the boy's youthful sharpness.

"Something is bothering you, Fargo. It is in your face," the boy said.

Fargo hesitated, but decided to answer. "You keep this between us, Miguel," he said, and the boy nodded happily at the idea of something conspiratorial. "Indian pony prints, fresh ones, all around us," Fargo said.

"Comanche?" Miguel whispered.

"More than likely." Fargo grimaced, glancing back to see Verna come into sight. Rosalie and Abby followed, and he let them see him nose the pinto downward through a stand of cottonwoods. The passage sloped more sharply, but the sides rose and he scanned the trees.

Miguel kept beside him. "You think they see us?" the boy asked.

"It's possible," Fargo grunted. He swept the forestland again, but he saw nothing move, no branches quiver. With Comanches, that didn't mean a lot, and he suddenly reined up as he heard the sounds from beyond a thick cluster of trees ahead of them. Miguel's eyes went to him at once, wide with questions. "No, that's not them. Too much noise," Fargo said, and he moved forward carefully as the three young women came up. He put a finger to his lips as he glanced back at them and nosed the Ovaro through the trees.

The sound grew louder, then took form and became voices, grunted words in Spanish. He dismounted, motioned for the girls to stay still, and crept forward on foot and found Miguel beside him. He saw the figures come into sight through the trees, six horsemen, most wearing sombreros with cartridge belts slung across their chests. A small canvas-topped wagon followed the six horsemen, driven by an older, fat-bellied figure.

The Trailsman backed away silently, Miguel scurrying alongside him, and reached the spot where the three girls waited.

"What is it?" Verna asked.

"*Pistoleros,*" Miguel said, and pulled himself onto the mule.

"Mexican bandits who move back and forth across the border," Fargo explained. "This way. Move slowly." He sent the Ovaro up onto a slope, where he spied a dense stand of trees and high brush that bore tiny yellow flowers. He halted and motioned for the others to cluster close together in the dense foliage. He could plainly hear the *pistoleros* as they slowly made their way down the slope, and he caught a glimpse of their canvas-topped wagon. His eyes moved up from the wagon, scanned the opposite slope, and he cursed in silence as he discerned the dark shapes amid the trees, silent and motionless. Everybody's come to the party, he thought.

The sound snapped into the air next to him as Abby sneezed—once, then twice, then three times before she could stop herself. He saw the expression of dismay flood her face as she barely managed to stifle another sneeze. "These yellow flowers," she gasped.

Fargo peered through the trees and saw the Mexicans were already coming toward them.

"Run, that way," he ordered, and pointed downhill.

Verna pulled her horse around first and the others followed, Miguel on the jenny last in line. They would only get halfway down the hill before the bandits picked them up, Fargo knew, and he drew back deeper into the thicket of cottonwoods. He could see the bandits clearly now as they swerved, chasing the girls downhill, and it was but moments later when he heard their shouts of triumph.

His eyes went to the hills and quickly found the silent horsemen there. The Comanche hadn't moved, motionless shadows watching the scene below, and Fargo grunted in satisfaction. They had done exactly as he'd expected, and he moved carefully forward to peer through the trees.

The bandits had halted in a clearing a few dozen yards downhill, now with Verna, Rosalie, Abby, and Miguel herded together. They chattered excitedly among themselves as they pulled the girls from their horses.

"Take your hands off me," Abby flung at one, a short, heavyset man with a pencil-thin mustache. He laughed, reached out, and grasped her breast. She swung, caught him across the face with a hard slap, and he stopped laughing.

One of the others stepped forward, seized Abby by

one arm, and half-spun her around as the heavyset one smashed her across the side of the head. Abby fell face-forward, lay still for a moment, and then slowly pushed to her feet. Two of the others were holding Rosalie, one pulling the buttons of her blouse open and staring with delight at her ample gifts. Fargo saw Miguel rush to Verna's aid as she was yanked forward and receive a blow for it that sent him rolling a dozen feet across the ground.

"Bastards," Verna shouted.

"Tie the little *cacahuete* up," the short one ordered, and Fargo saw one of the others wrap a lariat around Miguel's still-dazed form.

Rosalie had been stripped to the waist and the others gathered around, touching, admiring, shouting crude compliments.

Fargo swore silently, but he had expected as much. If he had tried to run with them, he'd be down there, too, or they'd know he was running loose somewhere near and they'd be alert and searching for him. But they'd not be the only ones to know that, he grimaced. The silent, shadowed observers on the hill would have seen him, too. For now they didn't know about him, either, and that was even more important.

"We take them one at a time," the short man shouted, and the others chorused agreement. He leered at Rosalie. "We start with this one. Tie the other two up for now," he said.

Fargo saw the canvas-covered wagon had been halted at one side of the clearing, and the older, fat-bellied man leapt down to join the others. He ogled Rosalie with grinning anticipation as the rest of her clothes were stripped from her. She faced the Mexicans with her full-figured nakedness, pride and defiance mixed in her stance.

Fargo swore silently again and his hand tightened on

the butt of the Colt at his side. He had taken the gamble. The truth was he'd little choice but to take it. He'd depended on timing, on the ways of the Comanche, on knowing that they would wait for the right moment of surprise. But perhaps he'd counted on too many little things working with perfect timing and now it wasn't going as planned. He couldn't let the men have their way with Rosalie. He had run out of waiting time. He had to act, even though it would tear apart what he'd hoped to let happen.

"Grab her arms," he heard the short *pistolero* order, and two of the others seized Rosalie, flung her to the ground on her back. The others, laughing and cheering, gathered around her prostrate form, and Fargo glimpsed the ringleader start to yank his trousers open. The Trailsman started to draw the Colt, flung a glance at the hill, and held the curse back as the shadowed shapes moved and became lithe, black-haired riders on surefooted Indian ponies, most holding their short bows with arrows already resting on bowstrings. They moved slowly, at first, then suddenly raced downhill.

Fargo dropped his Colt back into its holster. At last, he grunted silently. It was happening, the sequence of events he had counted on. The Comanche had simply been more careful than he'd expected. They had waited to make certain their target was fully preoccupied, and now they were racing to strike, making full use of surprise and speed.

With no danger now of the Comanche spotting him from the hills, Fargo stepped forward where he could see the entire clearing. The *bandidos* were busy cheering on their short, stocky leader as he lowered himself over Rosalie. By the time they heard the Comanche and tried to turn, a hail of arrows had already hurtled into half of them. Some of the others managed to draw their guns before a second hail of arrows cut them down. The short one leapt up from Rosalie, still hanging out of his trousers, tried to draw his gun when two arrows slammed deep into his belly.

He collapsed at once, Fargo noticed, and he saw that Rosalie had managed to pull on her skirt. The Comanche dismounted and Fargo had a chance to count. Eight of them, he grimaced, the leader a sharp-eyed, lithe figure wearing a soiled yellow kerchief around his neck, army trousers, and a deerskin vest. He stepped to Rosalie, walked around her as though he were buying a steer at an auction, and with a sudden motion flung her against one of the other braves and barked orders. The Comanche spoke the Shoshonean language, and Fargo knew enough to understand the command, though the Indian's actions were clear enough without words. Rosalie was tied to the wagon beside Verna with a lariat taken from one of the dead Mexicans.

The Comanche turned to the lifeless forms on the ground and began to pick over each. The Comanche believed in being practical, and they methodically removed rings, bracelets, hairbrushes, boots, and of course, guns and cartridges. Fargo watched them go about their task with the grim efficiency of vultures, tossing each body into the brush when they finished with it. But they had taken care of the *pistoleros,* done half his work for him. Now he had to face only eight Comanches, hardly an appealing prospect, yet the best of a bad bargain. He brought his eyes to Rosalie, Verna, and Abby and saw the despair in their faces. By now they were thinking that he had decided to save his own neck. He couldn't blame them for the thought. Most men would have fled, but he was not most men, a fact that he had learned was sometimes more of a burden than a blessing.

He returned his eyes to the Comanche as they began to climb into the canvas-covered wagon, and he heard their shouts of glee first, then he saw their arms holding whiskey casks as they clambered out. The wagon had obviously been a prize the Mexicans had seized somewhere, and Fargo felt the excitement stir inside him as he watched the Comanche open the casks and immediately begin to gulp down the whiskey. Shouts of delight mingled with loud belching, and Fargo watched one of the braves walk to Rosalie to check her bonds. He quickly checked Verna and Abby, and satisfied they were securely bound, he gave Miguel a kick as he returned to the whiskey casks.

The others were already on their way to becoming thoroughly drunk. The Comanche practicality surfacing again, Fargo nodded. They had much more of a chance to get their hands on a woman than on good whiskey.

Their captives bound, they'd be there when the whiskey was gone. It was time to enjoy the fire brew the white man denied them, and they went at it with headlong delight. Fargo allowed a grim smile to touch his lips. The whiskey wagon had become a way and a means, turning an uncertain and very dangerous task into an avenue of unexpected opportunity.

The Trailsman glanced at the sun where it was vanishing over the mountain. The Comanche would be passed out before the night was over, and he settled back to wait, suddenly able to enjoy the luxury of hope. He watched the dusk become night and the moon rise to illuminate the clearing with its pale light. Below, the Comanche were still drinking, but the wild laughter had turned to slurred, disconnected words. He waited, and finally the last two Indians keeled over and the only sound was that of drunken snoring.

He let another half-hour go by to make certain they

were all in the heavy sleep of drunkenness and then he started down the hill, the Ovaro following at his heels. When he reached the edge of the clearing, he left the horse and moved into the open alone. The Comanche had consumed enough whiskey to keep the ordinary man asleep for an entire night. But they, too, were not ordinary men. They were Comanche, made of the wild sensitivity of the land they had made part of themselves. He'd not risk carelessness, not even with drunken Comanche, and he crossed the clearing on silent steps.

Abby saw him first, her eyes widening as a gasp of surprise fell from her lips that reached Verna and then Rosalie. He saw little Miguel push to his feet as he came to a halt in front of the wagon.

"Oh, God, we thought—" Verna began, and he interrupted in a curt whisper.

"I know what you thought," he said, reached down to the narrow calf holster around his leg, and drew out the thin, double-edged throwing knife, both sides razor-sharp. He cut Miguel's bonds first, then freed Abby, Verna, and Rosalie. The *pistoleros* had put their horses at the far end of the clearing, and the Comanche had left them untouched. Fargo swept the eight figures stretched out where they had toppled in a ragged circle, the emptied whiskey casks strewn among them. He spoke in a whisper just loud enough for Abby and the others to hear. "Go to your horses and stay there. Don't try riding away," he said, and drew a frown from everyone, "Drunk or not, I'm betting they'll come awake if you try to ride off," he said, glancing at the prone figures again. "They won't be in good shape, but they'll come after you and you'd be surprised how fast anger will sober them up. They'll have the advantage again, and everything that's happened will be wasted."

'So what do we do?" Rosalie asked.

"You stay by your horses and wait there for me. I'm going to spook them and their ponies at the same time," Fargo said. "Now move, very slowly and very quietly." He watched as Verna started off first; Rosalie paused to scoop up her blouse and then Abby and Miguel followed. Turning, he made his way back to where he'd left the Ovaro and led the horse in a circle around the clearing until he reached the far end where the others waited. He handed Verna the Ovaro's reins. "Hold him here with you," he said, and swept everyone with a hard glance. "You stay here, no matter what you see, until I get here."

Verna nodded for everyone and Fargo left again, moved into the clearing, and found the Comanche ponies clustered together a few yards from their whiskey-sotted masters. He dropped into a crouch as one of the Indians groaned, sat half-upright, and fell back again.

Fargo moved on to where the canvas-topped wagon sat, then went around to the rear and peered inside. Three empty burlap sacks and a broken chicken crate were the only things in the wagon, and he quickly tossed the burlap sacks over the crate, lit a match and set the burlap on fire. He waited until the flames began to leap upward to reach the canvas top of the wagon. The old canvas caught fire at once.

Fargo backed from the rear of the wagon, ran to the front, and vaulted onto the driver's seat. He wheeled the wagon in a tight circle, snapped the reins hard on the horse, and the animal went into a gallop. He hugged the edge of the clearing as the horse raced off at full speed, half-panicked by the sudden heat and the flame behind him. The wagon careened around the edge of the clearing, the racing horse creating a backdraft of wind that whipped the flames until the entire back of the wagon was afire.

The Indian ponies bucked and raced off in all directions as the flaming wagon charged at them, and Fargo saw the Comanche wake, sit up, and stare into the night. What they saw through their bleary eyes was a flaming apparition, a fiery cone racing toward them out of the darkness. Fargo saw them run, some diving away, others screaming in terror, but all fleeing, their reactions fashioned of whiskey, surprise, and the myths and beliefs that were part of their culture. For the first few explosive moments it seemed that the fire spirit had flung a huge fireball upon them. They would realize the truth soon enough, but not before he could get the women to safety.

Fargo felt the heat of the flames searing his back, the wood of the wagon burning fiercely now. He dropped forward, reached onto the drive shaft, and unhitched the horse. As the animal raced away, Fargo jumped from the wagon. He saw the fiery wagon still rolling fast, headed for the trees, and he raced in a low crouch to where the girls waited with the horses.

"Ride," he hissed as he vaulted onto the ovaro and led the way down another slope. He took a passage that turned left and rose upward, and when he came to a plateau, he raced west, keeping the pace until he finally slowed after almost a half-hour of riding. He brought the pinto to a walk and let Miguel catch up on the jenny, then moved through a stand of spruce. He halted at a level stretch of land where the last of the moonlight still shone. "We'll bed down here till morning," he said. "Try to get some sleep."

"That won't be hard for me," Rosalie said as she sank to the ground.

Fargo took his bedroll and moved into the spruce, drawing a deep breath as he lay down. The Comanche would have a hard time finding their ponies, he was certain. To go back to camp on foot would be an even greater humiliation. It had gone well, Fargo admitted to himself, but he refused to embrace complacency as he fell asleep. Not with the Comanche. Not ever.

When morning came, to his surprise and delight, he found a stand of rich muscadine grapes, and they served as breakfast for everyone.

"My stomach is still in knots," Verna said as she ate lightly. "I'm sorry for what I thought yesterday, Fargo. I apologize."

"Me, too," Rosalie said. "I shouldn't have thought it either."

He looked at Abby, who returned his glance with a cool stare. "I'm sorry I misjudged you, but it was a perfectly reasonable conclusion under the circumstances. I won't apologize for it," she said.

"Little hardnose, aren't you?" Fargo said.

"I believe in being honest," Abby returned.

"I'm all for honesty," Fargo said, finished his grapes, and climbed onto the Ovaro. "Let's ride," he said, and turned toward the higher hills that formed part of the Alegrosa Mountain.

Miguel rode alongside Fargo as they rode north to return to the area where Yancey had done his last robbery. He pushed the Overo a dozen yards ahead of Miguel, and his eyes swept the hills with their thick stands of cottonwoods. He reined up sharply as he saw a low branch move. He backed the Ovaro into a clump of high brush, his eyes riveted on the spot where the branch had quivered. He had to wait only seconds when the horseman came out of the trees, the Comanche with the dirty yellow kerchief.

Fargo started to draw the Colt when Miguel rode past on the jenny. Fargo swore silently as the Comanche whirled at once. Miguel tried to bring the mule to a halt, but the Comanche had seen him and raced toward him, a long-bladed hunting knife in one hand. He had found one of the ponies and had come searching. Had he been the only one? There was no time to stay back and find out. The Comanche was almost upon Miguel as the boy tried to turn the jenny around and she balked in typical mule fashion.

Fargo raised the revolver, took fast aim, and fired just as the Comanche started to bring the knife down in a slashing motion. The bullet caught the Indian in the side of the neck and his head made sudden bucking motions as he flew forward, hit the mane of his pony, and toppled to the ground with his knife arm still upraised.

Fargo sent the pinto out of the trees and saw Miguel look up at him with eyes round as saucers. "Get out of here," Fargo hissed at the boy as he leaned over and helped him yank the mule's head around.

Miguel started back to meet Verna, who came into sight, Rosalie and Abby close behind her. The sound of the jenny's hooves smothered the faint swish of the arrow until it had almost reached its mark. Fargo had time only to half-twist in the saddle as the shaft grazed his upper arm. He fell sideways out of the saddle as another arrow hurtled past his head. He landed on his shoulder and felt the Colt skitter out of his hand. He rolled, glimpsed another Comanche racing at him, a third one coming up behind. The nearest one had another arrow on his bowstring and let it fly, and Fargo rolled again and felt the shaft slam into the dirt alongside him.

He managed to get to his feet as the Indian whirled his pony around, but the third brave was at him, leaning low in the saddle to swipe viciously at him with a tomahawk. Fargo ducked and the tomahawk grazed the top of his head, but as the Indian charged past, Fargo flung himself forward, one long arm outstretched. He closed his hand around the Indian's wrist and the man flew from the pony. He hit the ground hard on the side of his head, grunted in pain, then tried to rise unsteadily, but Fargo kicked out, the blow catching the man in the small of his back. The Indian fell forward, the tomahawk hitting the ground, and Fargo had only time to dive aside as the third brave came at him again. The Indian's arrow missed and Fargo closed his hand around the tomahawk, rose to one knee, and let the Comanche whirl his pony around again. He saw the Indian drop the bow and reach into his waistband for a six-gun, probably taken from one of the *pistoleros*.

Still charging atop his pony, the Comanche fired wildly, plainly not too familiar with guns. Fargo ducked, let him race by, then pull his pony to a halt and start to turn. The Indian had almost turned around when Fargo flung the tomahawk with all his strength and saw the heavy blade fly end over end to smash into the man's chest. The Comanche quivered on the horse, the blade embedded almost to the handle in his chest. He reached up with both hands to grasp the handle, but his face contorted and a spray of red fell from his mouth. His hands were still wrapped around the handle of the tomahawk when he hit the ground with a lifeless thud. As his hands finally dropped away to fall on the ground, Fargo saw the other brave pulling himself to his feet. The Indian turned to him, backed away, and suddenly flung himself to his right. Fargo saw his hands reaching out for the Colt on the ground and started for the brave, but he saw he was too late as the man's hand closed around the gun. He cursed as he saw the Comanche whirl, half on his back, and bring the Colt up when a shot exploded, sending up a cloud of dirt some six inches from the Indian. Fargo glanced behind him and saw Rosalie holding a big Joslyn army revolver with both hands. She fired again and the gun bucked as her shot missed by more than the first one had.

Startled, the Comanche began to turn to fire at Rosalie, but the precious seconds were enough time for Fargo to leap forward, twist with both legs outstretched, and slam into the Indian with both feet. The man fell backward as the Colt went off into the air, and before he could bring the gun around, Fargo, palms pressed into the ground, kicked out again, and the blow caught the Indian on the point of his jaw. The Colt again went off into the air as the man's finger pressed against the trigger. Fargo leapt to his feet, reached the Comanche in one long stride, and his powerful hand closed around the man's wrist, twisted it, and the Colt fell to the ground. Fargo seized hold of it and saw the Indian dive at him, teeth bared, hands outstretched. Fargo only half-raised the Colt and fired, and the Comanche's chest exploded as he fell on his face.

The Trailsman rose, spun the chamber of the Colt, and looked down at the lifeless form. "Hate a man who wastes bullets, especially if they're mine," he muttered, and straightened as he strode back to where Rosalie lowered the gun. "Thanks," he said, and eyed the big Joslyn. "That the gun you used to stampede Otis' herd?" he asked casually.

"That's the gun I keep in my traveling bag," she said stiffly.

He smiled as he reloaded the Colt. "Better put it back there. It might come in handy again sometime," he said, and she stuffed the pistol back into her canvas bag. Her eyes went to the slain Comanche.

"These three found their ponies," he said. "I thought it might happen."

"And the others?" she asked.

"Walking back to their camp," Fargo said.

"How do you know they didn't find their ponies?" Verna questioned.

"They'd have been with these three if they had," Fargo replied as he pulled himself onto the Ovaro. "Now let's ride. There's plenty of good daylight left."

He sent the pinto north again until he had returned close to the area where Tom Yancey had done his last robbery. He halted, his lake-blue eyes sweeping the hills that were part of Alegrosa Mountain.

"His damn cabin could be anywhere in these hills. We could search for months and not find it," Verna said.

"It wouldn't be anywhere," Fargo remarked, and they stared at him. "I can write off three-quarters of these hills," he said, and slowly moved the pinto forward at a walk.

"How?" Abby asked.

"This cabin was a hiding place long before Tom Yancey took sick. That means he wouldn't put it just anywhere. It had to be high enough to let him see all around. It wouldn't be backed against a steep hill where he'd have to run up if he had unexpected company. It'd be someplace where he could run down any side to get away," Fargo said while he continued to sweep the hills with a searching gaze. "And it'd be near water, a stream most likely. A man wouldn't put a hideout cabin where he'd have to travel to get water. And there'd be the trees, of course," Fargo said.

"The trees?" Abby echoed.

"He wouldn't put a hideout cabin in a stand of black walnut, hackberry, cottonwood, or shadbush where it'd been seen when they shed their leaves, come fall. It'd be among evergreens, Western spruce, white fir, piñon pine," Fargo said, and caught the admiration that lay in Abby's eyes as she watched him. He returned his gaze to the hills, letting his eyes move back and forth in long, slow sweeps. And suddenly he caught the flash of sunlight on water. His eyes narrowed as he peered at the trees high on one of the distant hills. "Piñon pine and a stream," he muttered.

"Where?" Verna asked with excitement in her voice.

"Way up there," he said, pointing, and sent the Ovaro forward. The others fell into line behind him as he made his way up through passages that were both steep and narrow. He saw the mountain stream skipping downhill through the trees, and his eyes narrowed as he took in the way the terrain sloped down on all sides. He threaded the pinto through a thick stand of pine and reined to a halt, letting the others come up alongside him as he stared at the small log cabin with the sod base.

"Bull's-eye," he said over Rosalie's gasp, Verna's yelp of excitement, and Abby's slow hiss of approval.

# 5

The closed, silent cabin seemed to stare back at them as though it were an ancient Egyptian sphinx, implacable, unfathomable, waiting with silent secrets.

Abby was the first to dismount. "Let's go see," she said, and started to stride to the cabin.

"Hold on," Fargo said, and swung to the ground. "I'll go first. Yancey might have rigged up something. It wouldn't be past him."

Abby halted and Fargo moved to the cabin, walked around it, then stepped back and scanned the edge of the roof, letting his eyes move up and down the sides of the closed door. When he moved forward again, he halted at the side of the door, drew his foot back, and kicked. The door swung open with a creak, and he paused, peered into the cabin, and then stepped inside. He waved back and Abby was first to reach him as he stood in the center of the cabin and surveyed the single room.

A puncheon table took up one corner, a narrow cot lay against one wall, and two straight-backed wood chairs and a row of shelves with trenchers and wooden cups filled another wall. Clothes were stacked neatly on the lower shelves, and two water buckets stood on their ends in a corner. All in all it was a neat cabin, Fargo concluded.

Abby's voice broke into his thoughts. She was at the table, staring down at a folded sheet of parchment. "Look here," she cried out. "To Verna Simpson, Abby Tillstrom, and Rosalie Hodges."

Rosalie and Verna hurried to the table as Abby picked up the piece of parchment and unfolded it. "Read it," Rosalie said excitedly.

" 'If you are reading this, it means you have found your way here,' " Abby began. " 'If only one or two of you have reached here, it will do you no good. You must all be together, all three of you. If that is so, you have taken the first step toward finding the money, but only the first step. The rest is for you to figure out.

" 'There is a lot of money. I had a good time taking it. Those I robbed could, for the most part, afford it. A lot of them deserved robbing. You three young ladies were good to me, each in your own way. But no one should be given anything. One must work for one's rewards. Being a highwayman is work. Let no one tell you differently. I leave you one more clue. No one of you can find it alone. Seek and maybe ye shall find. Yours with a smile, Tom Yancey.' "

Abby lowered the sheet of parchment, the message on it written in a careful, neat script, and her glance went to Verna. "What's it mean?" she asked, and the other young woman shrugged helplessly.

"Why can't any of us find it alone?" Abby pressed.

"I think he's telling us that it's so well hidden that it'll take all three of us to find it," Verna said.

"That must be it," Rosalie agreed. "He writes how you have to work for your rewards. He expects we'll have to work hard and together."

Abby's eyes went to Fargo. "You agree?"

"No. Yancey wouldn't be saying anything that simple. It's not his style," Fargo said.

"Then what do you think he means?" Rosalie frowned.

"Don't know," Fargo said. "I'd have to think more on it."

"Then I say we start by going over every inch of this cabin," Verna said.

"It's not here. That wouldn't be Yancey's style, either," Fargo said.

"Why not?" Abby asked.

"This was a hideout, but men have been caught in hideouts. Yancey knew that. He wouldn't keep the money with him so they could get him and the money at once. That'd leave him with nothing to bargain with," Fargo answered.

"Maybe he did, though. It's clear he wasn't like anyone else," Verna said.

"That's true," Fargo conceded.

"I still say we go over this place with a fine-tooth comb," Verna said, and Rosalie and Abby murmured agreement.

"Help yourself." Fargo shrugged and watched as Rosalie took one corner of the cabin, Abby and Verna started on the shelves, and Miguel poked into whatever he could reach. He leaned back, waited, and saw night descend, then lighted the two kerosene lamps in the cabin.

Finally, after every inch of the interior of the cabin had been searched, Rosalie called a halt. "Tomorrow we go over the walls, the roof, every log and stone in this place," she said.

"I'll bring you in some beef strips and then I'll bed down outside," Fargo said, and after he'd shared the meal with everyone, he put his bedroll down a dozen yards from the cabin. He had undressed to his under-drawers when he heard the cabin door open and the slender form slip outside, peer into the darkness, and finally find him. Abby approached, clothed in a short cotton nightgown that revealed the thin yet shapely calved legs, the smallish breasts touching little points in the top of the fabric.

"Have trouble sleeping?" he slid at her.

"Some things I want to say," she murmured, and he saw her eyes move across his almost naked body. "I'm not like Rosalie or Verna. I know you think I'm cold—a hardnose, I believe you said."

"Hardnose is one thing. Cold's another," he remarked.

She shrugged away the distinction. "What are you going to do, come tomorrow?" she asked. "You've done what we hired you to do, find the cabin. You can go your way now."

"You asking if that's what I'm going to do?" he pushed back at her.

"I'm saying I'll understand if you do," Abby said. "And I'm grateful for all you've done."

"More honesty?"

"I guess so. It's something I wanted to say."

"Fair enough," he said. "You don't have to go back to the cabin, you know."

The coolness came quickly to her eyes. "I told you, I'm not like Rosalie and Verna," she said.

"Maybe your honesty doesn't go as far as theirs," he said.

He expected a sharp answer, he knew he'd pushed her to one, but she surprised him. "Maybe not," she said thoughtfully, and reached one hand out, touched the muscled symmetry of his chest, then moved slowly down to the hard abdomen. "Maybe not," she echoed, and turned and hurried back to the cabin.

He lay down on the bedroll and slept quickly in the cool and soft night, and when he woke, the new morning sun was a warm touch on his body. He washed in the stream that ran alongside the rear of the cabin. He was dressed when Verna emerged from the cabin, a towel over her shoulder as she made for the stream. Rosalie followed and then Abby, and he stepped inside the cabin, where Miguel waited in only trousers. He peered at the log walls, ran his hand slowly over the middle logs, traced a path around the cabin, and then knelt down to the base logs at the floor. Again, he slowly felt along each log with his hands until he rose, his lips pursed. He hadn't found even one that was loose. But he'd say nothing. They wouldn't be satisfied until they'd gone over the entire cabin, roof and stone base. And maybe they'd find a loose stone that was a hiding place. He couldn't rule it out entirely, not with Tom Yancey.

He stepped outside as he heard them returning from the stream. "I'll find us some breakfast," he said. "You can reach the roof by standing on a chair or one of the buckets." He walked away and caught the quiet greeting in Abby's glance. He let his thoughts wander as he walked through the trees. He'd revised his thinking about Tom Yancey. He'd not played a last, bitter joke on the three girls. The money was there for them someplace, and he had given them a way to find it. But he'd made it damn near impossible for them to find that way. That was the nature of his bizarre last gesture. It was a salve to his conscience, yet it was also one more last laugh at the world. Fargo realized he was beginning to understand Tom Yancey, and the appeal the man had held for so many. Most bandits and killers robbed and despoiled out of greed, but Tom Yancey's life had been one long laugh at the world.

Tom had spent a lifetime at it, each act striking out in his own strange and unique way. He couldn't commit an ordinary robbery. A commonplace holdup was beyond him. There always had to be that gesture, that bizarre twist that made it a cry inside a laugh. And in his last gesture, even though it was one of gratefulness, he couldn't change the pattern of his ways. The gesture had to be cloaked in his wry and strange ways, that bitterness he couldn't shed.

Fargo let the thoughts drift away, but his eyes were narrowed. He understood more of Tom Yancey now, but could that understanding help unravel the puzzle the man had left Rosalie, Verna, and Abby? He'd see if it could, he decided, his own sense of frustration and curiosity pushing him.

He turned off further thoughts as he found a thick cluster of high-bush cranberry. He took off his jacket and laid it on the ground, filled it with the sweet-sour red berries, and carried it back to the cabin, where everyone halted their searching to eat breakfast. The cold stream water tasted as fine as wine with the berries, and when breakfast ended, the searchers returned to their task, with Miguel lending a helping hand.

It didn't take long to go over the small cabin, and finally Rosalie slumped down on the ground, a glower wreathing her round face. "Nothing," she muttered. "Everything's solid as rock."

Verna and Abby came to sit down nearby and Fargo met Abby's narrowed glance. "You were right, of course," she said without bitterness. "What next?"

"We leave. There's nothing here that'll help you any except for the note, which you've read," Fargo said.

"Go where?" Verna questioned.

"Back to where he did his last job, for starters," Fargo said.

"What'll that tell us?" Abby asked.

"I don't know," Fargo admitted. "But maybe we'll come onto something. Maybe somebody saw him, a placer miner, an old mountain man. Or maybe I can pick up a trail, though that's damn unlikely. But sitting here won't get you anything."

"I guess not," Verna agreed.

"There's one more thing," Fargo offered. "Something he didn't even mention in that note he left you."

"The tattoos," Abby breathed.

"Exactly, which makes me think they're the key to it, somehow. I've learned to think the way Yancey did, in his roundabout way," Fargo said.

"They're exactly alike. What do they mean?" Rosalie asked.

"I don't have that answered yet, but you can bet they mean something," Fargo said. "Let's see yours again, Abby. It'll be quicker and easier than the others," he added blandly, and drew frowns from Rosalie and Verna. Abby lifted her skirt and turned the back of her knee for him to see. He peered at the strange tattoo, the two sides of the narrow pyramid and the tiny squares along the bottom. "Damned if I can figure it," Fargo murmured, and Abby let her skirt fall back in place. "Think, dammit, he must've said something when he did them."

"Only that it would help me find the hidden money," Rosalie said.

"Just what he said to me," Verna added, and Fargo glanced at Abby.

"All he said to me was that I had nice knees," she answered.

"He wanted us to have it. I say that means he

wanted to be sure each of us would look for the same thing. Maybe it's a sign he left someplace," Verna suggested.

"Not in this damn cabin," Rosalie snapped.

"No," Fargo said. "That'd be too direct for Tom Yancey. Get your gear together and let's ride. You can each think about it on the way." He turned and began to put his bedroll on the pinto as the others hurried into the cabin. They moved quickly, and soon he led the way down the second level of foothills, for the most part in silence.

It was midday when they reached the low foothills, and Fargo halted in a shady spot. As the others rested, he clambered onto a ledge that provided a clear view of the low range where the tree cover grew sparse and the red sandstone rock dominated.

He surveyed the terrain for any signs of movement, a mountain man with a burro, the wisp of a trail fire, a lean-to hastily constructed, or a long tom that would mean a streambed mining operation. But he saw nothing and returned to the others. They continued the trip downward almost to the bottom of the low hills before darkness began to slide over the land.

Fargo caught an antelope jackrabbit for fresh meat and a pair of scrawny shadbush provided a spot to make camp. Miguel helped find wood for a fire, and when the meal was finished, Fargo leaned back and let his eyes move across the three young women. They had eaten in silence, plainly upset at what increasingly seemed like an impossible quest. But he admitted to a mild stir of resentment at Rosalie and Verna, and he decided to give it voice.

"You girls seem to be taking something for granted," he said. "Except for Abby."

"What do you mean?" Verna frowned.

"I've finished my job for you. I could be on my way. Abby had the good manners to tell me she recognized that," he said.

Verna's mouth tightened and she cast a quick glance at Rosalie. "It's not bad manners on our part," she murmured. "It's fear. We were afraid to bring it up."

He turned the reply in his mind for a moment and realized that it was most likely honest. "All right, I'll accept that," he said.

"Will you stay to help?" Rosalie asked.

"Seems I am," Fargo grunted. "Curiosity is a damn powerful force."

He saw Verna's sigh of relief. "Thank you," she said. "Without you we might as well give up. We can't come up with anything, not about the tattoo or about what the note meant or anything else."

"None of us can find it alone, he said that much in the note. I still say that means it's someplace that'll take a lot of work to get at, more than one person could do, such as maybe in some abandoned mine," Rosalie insisted.

Fargo shrugged but inwardly dismissed the explanation. It was logical, and logical moves were not part of Tom Yancey. Yet he had nothing better to offer, and he put out the fire and took down his bedroll. Everyone found a niche to sleep inside the rock-bound area.

He was up first when morning came, and he saw Abby asleep nearby. The bottom of the short nightgown had slid upward as she slept and he saw thighs that were as nicely curved as her calves despite their thinness. He washed with his canteen, dressed, and surveyed the low hills again as the others woke and prepared to ride.

Miguel rode beside him as they moved downhill and his thin, eager face showed that it was still all a great adventure to him, the money no more than an abstract prize. Any goal would have done as well for him.

Fargo smiled to himself. Maybe that was the best way to take the whole thing, Fargo reflected, though a glance at Rosalie's frowning face told him he'd have a hard time selling her that approach.

It was late morning when they had almost reached the road where Tom Yancey had done his last robbery. Fargo pulled to a halt as he saw the spiral of dust rise, then the horsemen come into sight along the rise in the road. Seven, he counted, led by a man wearing a black jacket and a string tie. Fargo waited as Verna and Abby halted alongside him, Rosalie just behind them with Miguel.

The horsemen approached at a fast canter and slowed as they reached him, the man in the black jacket holding up one hand. "Well, now, this will make my morning," the man said with a smile. He had a clean-shaven face and was somewhere in his early thirties, Fargo guessed, and he had dark eyes and an authoritative way about him. "I'm Jim Halpin. I'd guess you're Fargo," the man said.

"You'd guess right," Fargo nodded.

Jim Halpin's eyes went to the three young women, and he flashed another cordial smile. "And these must be the three young ladies Tom Yancey took such a liking to," he said. Fargo felt the stir of surprise inside himself. "How'd you learn all this?" he asked, and swept the others with a quick, sharp glance. They were younger, most with the same clean-cut faces, serious yet not grim.

"It's my business to learn things. I'm a Pinkerton man, chief of the agency's southwest branch. These men are all Pinkerton agents," Halpin said. "We heard that Tom Yancey died in a doctor's office and that he told the doc he'd left all his money to three young ladies. Then we stopped at Gil Breaker's place and he told us about your visit. I knew you'd be around here someplace."

Fargo allowed a polite smile. "I still don't see how this affects you any," he said.

"A lot of the money Yancey stole belonged to clients of the agency. We say that Tom Yancey has no right to give anybody any of that money, not even to three such charming beneficiaries," Jim Halpin said. "The money is ours, stolen from our clients, and we expect to get it back to them."

"You have your name on any of that money? Got the coins stamped or the paper marked?" Fargo asked mildly, and the Pinkerton man's eyes narrowed. "Truth is you can't tell which of the money is yours. Seems to me you've no real claim to anything. Seems to me these gals have a right to whatever Tom Yancey wanted to leave them."

"We'll let a judge decide that," Halpin said. "Meanwhile did you find the money?"

"No," Verna said firmly.

"But you're going to keep searching for it," the Pinkerton man said, and Verna nodded, the nod echoed by Abby and Rosalie.

"You've got to have some reason for thinking you can find it," Halpin said. "Something Yancey gave you or said to you."

"They're just optimists," Fargo cut in.

Halpin's smile was chiding. "That's why they hired somebody with your reputation."

"They also believe in the American principle that a man has the right to leave his money to whoever he damn pleases," Fargo said.

"His money, not money he stole from somebody

else," Halpin snapped, and Fargo said nothing further as another band of horsemen appeared on a low hill and came toward them. Five riders, he counted, none as well decked out as the Pinkerton men, and it was Halpin who spoke when the newcomers reached them. "Sam Schreiber," Jim said. "I guess I don't have to ask what brings you here."

"You don't," Sam said, and his eyes went to Fargo. "I'm from the Star Silver Mining Company. Damn near half the money Tom Yancey stole he stole from us. Raiding our payroll carriers was a favorite of his," he said. "I stopped in to see Gil Breaker and he told us about you and these three young ladies."

"Gil Breaker's real talkative," Fargo grunted.

"I suppose you're going to tell us that half Yancey's money is really yours," Verna said, irritation in her voice.

"That's exactly what I'm telling you, girl," Sam Schreiber said.

"Mr. Fargo thinks Yancey had a right to leave them the money," the Pinkerton man cut in.

"He can tell a judge that. They all can, after we have the money back," the mining company man growled.

"Seeing as how nobody has the money, that's all talk," Fargo said.

"Only, Yancey gave these gals some lead on the money," Sam said. "So where they go, we go."

"That's exactly how we see it," Jim Halpin said.

Fargo's eyes hardened and he took both men in with one glance. "I don't like being crowded, gents, and I don't aim to let that happen," he said. "Since neither of you has any official power, I hope you won't test my patience."

"Every sheriff and every judge knows about Pinkerton detectives, Fargo," Halpin said.

"They do, but you're just a private detective agency and Schreiber's grinding his company's ax," Fargo said. "Now, we'll be moving on and I hope you don't press me."

"Wouldn't think of it, but it's a free country. We can ride where we please," Jim said, and Sam grunted agreement.

"I've said my piece." Fargo smiled, motioned to the girls, and set off at a trot. He crossed the road, moved onto a stretch of open land, and glanced back to see Halpin and Schreiber still talking to each other. He caught Abby glance back also and anticipated her question. "They'll follow," he told her. "They think you know more than you do, and they'll follow."

Rosalie's voice cut in. "They're probably right about the money. It was all stolen in the first place," she said. "Maybe he didn't have the right to leave it to us, or to anybody."

"Maybe not," Fargo agreed. "You want to let it go at that, or do you want the money?"

"I want the damn money, at least my share of it," Verna said. "None of us will ever get a chance at that much money again. I want to keep looking for it."

"Then we've got to shake our new friends," Fargo said, and glanced back to see that the two bands of riders were moving after them. Staying plenty far back, though. He smiled.

"How do you expect to do that?" Abby asked.

"You think about Yancey and those tattoos. I'll think about losing our friends," Fargo said, and continued to move south across relatively open and flat land.

The girls rode in silence behind him, Miguel at his side, as he tried to find a way to shake the men that followed. He rode into the late afternoon when he spied the river in the distance, and he frowned. It was a tributary of the Gila, which coursed down from Arizona. He had taken cattle over it a number of times and had learned its unique character. The Crazy River it was called, a name that was very appropriate.

He cast a glance up and saw the long shadows of night start to slide across the sky. He called a halt at an open place where only a handful of yucca grew amid the rocks. He had some of the jackrabbit meat left over and added the dried beef strips to it to make a meal as Abby and the others gathered around. Before night fell, he saw the Pinkerton men and Schreiber's band spread out in a wide circle. "They've joined forces for convenience. They'll post lookouts in case we try to move by night."

"But we're not, I take it," Abby said.

"No, but tomorrow we're going to cross the Crazy River. It has that name because it's peaceful and calm at both ends and you can cross it easily at either spot, but for a mile in the middle it's a raging, white-water rapids," Fargo said.

"So they'll know we'll have to cross at either end and be there to follow," Verna said.

"Only we're going to cross at the part that can't be crossed while they are watching the two ends," Fargo said, and he saw the apprehensive glance Rosalie exchanged with Abby and Verna. "It's the only way we'll shake them," he said.

"How are we going to cross at a place that can't be crossed?" Verna asked.

"Haven't figured that out yet, but I'll work on it," Fargo said cheerfully, and Rosalie blinked back at him. He tossed her a smile and turned to Miguel. "Now, I've a job for you," he said. "In a few hours, you go to Halpin, the Pinkerton man. Let the lookouts see you and take you to him. You tell him that I'm going to cross the river."

"Tell him?" Miguel frowned.

"Yes, I want them to be sure. That way they'll position themselves to wait and watch at either end," Fargo said. "You go to him and say that you came along with the girls to make a dollar, but you haven't been paid anything. Tell him you've some information for him if he pays you for it. He'll believe you. He won't figure you as anything much more than a smartass little kid. After he pays you and you tell him, come back here. Have you got that now?"

"*Sí, sí.*" Miguel nodded.

"Tell him you had to wait until we were all asleep," Fargo added, and Miguel nodded again, excitement shining in his black-brown eyes. "Now lay down and take a nap," Fargo ordered as he took his bedroll down. He watched the girls lie down as they prepared to sleep, and the midnight moon was high in the night sky when he shook Miguel awake. The boy hurried away and Fargo lay back on his bedroll. It was a little less than an hour when he discerned the small form hurrying back. He sat up. Miguel dropped to the ground beside him, his thin face almost shining. "It went well. He believed me, just the way you said he would," Miguel told him. "And he gave me two dollars."

"Now everybody's happy," Fargo said. "I'll wager that when we wake in the morning they'll be gone. They'll leave before dawn to take up their positions on the the other side of the river. They'd like to give us the idea that they've gone their way." He lay back down and pressed Miguel's shoulder. "You did fine. Now get some sleep."

"*Sí*, Fargo." Miguel smiled happily. "Tomorrow we fool them. Tomorrow will be a good day."

"Definitely," Fargo said, and watched the boy hurry off to curl himself alongside Verna. A good day, he muttered silently. All he had to do was figure out how to cross a river where it couldn't be crossed.

# 6

"You were right, Fargo," Miguel chortled as he scanned the surrounding land in the new morning sun. "They are gone."

"Let's get moving ourselves," Fargo said, and Miguel ran to climb onto the jenny as the others pulled themselves together. Fargo led the way in a circle, away from the river and into a long stretch of hackberry that wound its way back to parallel the shoreline. He stayed in the trees, but he could catch glimpses of the river as they rode. As they passed the calm, almost sluggish lower stretch of the river, Fargo peered to the other shore but saw only the distant trees. Halpin and his men were in there, he was certain, spread out to cover as much of the section as possible. By now, Schreiber had his men positioned at the other end. Fargo frowned and continued to move slowly through the trees. As he moved left to skirt a dead tree, he found Verna at his side and he saw the frown that suddenly crossed her brow.

The sound had suddenly come to her, a low hiss that grew stronger, becoming a roar covered with a harsh hiss. Fargo moved the Ovaro to the left through the trees. The river came into clear view now, no longer a sluggish, slow channel of water but a leaping, roaring mass of swirling crosscurrents and cascades of spray where it struck against partly submerged rocks. White-water foam leapt high, and the angry sound matched the fury of the water. He saw Rosalie and Abby pull to a halt to stare with openmouthed astonishment.

"How does it suddenly become like this?" Abby gasped.

"I understand it has something to do with the conformation of the land at this stretch. There's a powerful undercurrent that comes downriver, and suddenly this stretch narrows and the bottom changes character. The current is squeezed and funneled, and the water takes on the speed of a runaway longhorn," he explained.

"We can't cross that. The horses could never make it," Verna murmured as she stared at the racing water.

Fargo dismounted, and as Abby and Rosalie frowned at him, he began to undress until he had only his drawers on. He folded his clothes, put them atop the Ovaro, and led the horse into a deep thicket of trees. He returned carrying his lariat and strode to the edge of the racing river.

"Dismount and put your horses with mine," he said as he scanned the water. Verna was first to return, Rosalie and Abby followed, and he caught Abby's eyes moving over the muscled symmetry of his near-naked torso. He peered across the raging foam of the white water, and his eyes narrowed as he took note of how the water flowed strongly to the right where it passed a wide rock. He calculated the speed of the water and the distance to a spot some twenty yards downriver on the opposite bank. Finally he turned back to the three young women and cut three lengths of rope from his lariat. He wrapped one around Rosalie's waist as a measure and, satisfied, handed the other two to Verna and Abby.

"You want to tell us what this is all about?" Verna asked as he began to wrap one end of his lariat around the base of a tree that grew almost to the river's edge.

"Everything in time," he said. "You've each got a thick canvas sack of extra clothes. Bring all three sacks here." They hurried back to the horses, and when they returned, he had the rope tightly secured around the tree and had dropped the rest of the lariat in a loose circle on the ground. "I'm going to go into the river," he said. "But I'm not fool enough to think I can swim against this current. Nobody could. But I'm going to hang on to this rope. It'll unwind as I'm carried downriver. By the way this water's flowing, it should carry me to the other shore about twenty yards downriver. I'll find a way to climb out with the rope and then come back opposite you on the other side."

"You'll tie the other end to a tree there to give us something to hang on to when we cross," Verna finished.

"That's right," Fargo said. "But before you start across, you wrap that length of rope around your waist and tie it onto the line. That way if you lose your grip—and you damn well may—you won't be swept away."

"We'll be soaking wet when we get to the other side," Abby said.

"You'll stay in the trees, take off your things, and let them dry out. I'm the only one who will need dry clothes. I'll be coming back to this side to finish sending our friends off on a wild-goose chase. I can't do it soaking wet," Fargo said.

"What about me, Señor Fargo?" Miguel asked almost plaintively.

"You'll stay right here and wait for me to come back across," Fargo said, and the boy nodded with relief.

"What about our sacks of clothing? Why did you want them?" Rosalie asked, and Fargo answered by tying the three sacks onto his body, one against his chest, another against his back, and the third around his crotch.

"Protection against the rocks," Verna said, and he nodded.

"I'm going to get slammed against them. There's no way I can avoid it," Fargo said. "I've got to go with the current."

Abby licked dryness from her lips. "What if you lose your grip on the rope?"

"You're on your own, ladies," he said.

"Maybe we should find another way to cross," Verna muttered.

"There is no other way," he bit out. "And no other way to shake the Pinkerton boys." He stepped toward the edge of the racing river, adjusted the sacks against his body, and started to move into the water when he heard Abby's call.

"Wait," she said, and hurried to him. She reached up, her lips touching his, a gentle, tender kiss, and then she pulled away. "For luck," she murmured.

"Better than a rabbit's foot." He grinned and stepped into the water. He held the end of the lariat clenched in one hand and wrapped it around his forearm three times. His feet went out from under him as though they'd been kicked away, and he was on his back, being turned, carried away in a sudden rush. He felt a spray of foam slam over him. He turned onto his stomach and felt the racing water seize him as though he were in the grip of a giant, invisible hand. He was pulled to one side, then a rip of current yanked him in the other direction. He slammed into the first rock, grunted at the force of it, and was grateful for the canvas sack against his back. A surge of water seized him, flipping him over, and he felt the rope cutting into his forearm as he clung on for dear life. He managed to bring his other hand up to grasp hold of the rope and take some of the cutting pressure from his right wrist and arm. He fought against the desire to resist the churning water, aware that to do so would only use up his strength, and he let himself turn and swing as he was carried.

But as another crosscurrent violently swung him around, he felt pain that almost numbed his forearm, and he cast a glance at the distant shore. It seemed beyond his reach as the raging rapids carried him downriver. His lips pulled back in pain as he side-swiped another rock, and he felt his shoulder and arm muscles begin to burn as his tendons and ligaments were stretched beyond endurance. But he glimpsed the wide rock as he swept past it and he realized he was being pushed with amazing speed toward the opposite shore. He heard himself cursing in pain as he clung to the rope, arm stretched to its very limits and the water turning him over and over as though he were a spinning top.

The sack against his chest took the force of the rock he slammed into, but because the wet sack had lost some of its resilience, the shock was greater than it had been from previous hits. "Damn," he heard himself swear as he felt the rope beginning to slip from his soaked fingers and forearm. He tried to close his hand tighter, but his cramped fingers refused to respond and the rope continued to inch through his grip. He cast a frantic glance to his left and saw the shoreline, close yet still too far to reach on his own. His lips pulled back and again he tried to stop the rope from slipping away from him. But the slippery wet lariat slowly continued to move, only a single turn still around his forearm.

A wild spray of foam rose up from a rock all but hidden below the racing water. Fargo drew his legs up and managed to smash into the rock with the sack across his chest. He grimaced in pain, but felt himself being tossed sideways and half out of the water. He twisted, saw the shoreline hardly more than a foot away, and drew his legs up again, kicked out sideways, and let the swirling water do the rest.

He was half on his back, still clinging to the rope as his feet touched the soft mud of the shore. He dug in, felt himself catch hold, and turned his body to sink down on one knee. He pulled forward, fighting against the pull of the water and crawled his way to the firmer ground of the shore. He fell forward onto the dry shore and drew in deep, racking gasps of air, then lay facedown, the rope clutched in his hand. He let his breath return before he lifted his head and pushed upward, still feeling the pain in his arm and shoulder. He climbed to his feet and began to walk back along the shoreline, and he came to a stop directly across from where the others clustered on the opposite shore.

Fargo took the end of the lariat, wrapped it around a tree trunk, and pulled on it until the rope was taut from shore to shore, hanging just above the racing water. He turned, faced the opposite shore, and waved furiously.

Verna was first to step forward, and he watched her tie the rope around her waist and then knot it around the tightly stretched line that crossed the raging rapids. Holding on to the taut rope with both hands, she lowered herself into the river and he saw her legs and lower torso instantly pulled straight. She began to pull herself slowly along the line, working her way across the leaping, clutching water. By the time she had reached the middle of the river he could see the agony in her face. She paused, clinging to the rope with both hands while the water pulled at her body, turned her half around, and lashed at her as though it were determined to have its victim.

Fargo dropped to one knee and called to her, words of encouragement and confidence, and slowly Verna began to again pull herself along the taut rope. The middle of the river lashed at her with its strongest current, twisting her body one way, then the other. Yet she clung, taking more time between each pull on the line, and finally she was within Fargo's reach. He leaned out, closed his hand over her left arm, and yanked her onto the shore. She lay on the bank, sobbing, soaked clothes clinging to her shaking body.

Fargo untied the rope around her waist and gave her time to stop shaking before he rose and peered across the river again. He motioned, and this time Rosalie stepped forward. She tightened the rope at her waist, secured herself to the taut ropeline, and plunged into the water with a determined abandon. Her legs were also instantly pulled straight by the rushing water, but Rosalie began to make her way along the line with rough energy. Fargo frowned at her as she quickly pulled herself along hand over hand, but she wasn't a quarter across the river when he saw her energy suddenly fade. She had expended too much energy too quickly. By the time she reached midriver she was clinging to the line with desperation, and he could see the fright on her round face. Fargo's lips pulled back in a grimace as he saw her hands slip from the ropeline.

The rushing, foaming water instantly turned her over, twisted her body in one direction, then swirled her in another. "The rope, dammit," he shouted. "Get hold of the rope."

Rosalie's arms flailed water and air as she was turned and pulled, and only the length of rope around her waist and attached to the lifeline stopped her from being swept to her death in the racing water.

"The rope," he shouted again. "Hold on to the rope." Rosalie continued to flail, go under, and come up again in the same spot, held there by her waist rope. She flung both arms up, and Fargo saw one hand close around the taut lifeline, then the other. She clung there, head lowered.

Verna's wet form appeared beside Fargo as he called to Rosalie's hanging figure. "Get your breath. Hang on," he said, and watched her cling to the rope, the river still tearing at her. But she held on and slowly slid one hand along the ropeline, then the other, moving with her eyes tightly closed as the water continued to buffet her until somehow, after what seemed like hours, she was close enough to reach.

Fargo seized hold of her, pulled her onto the shore, where she fell facedown gasping for air. "Take care of her," he said to Verna as he rose and motioned across the river to Abby. He swore silently. The trips were taking far longer than he'd expected, and he still had to make his way back. He didn't want the Pinkerton men to grow restless and come looking for them. He watched Abby plunge into the river as she held on to the taut ropeline, and though the racing water clutched and pulled at her at once, she moved toward him with more ease than any of the others had shown. She was lighter and leaner and, he saw, pound for pound stronger. She moved steadily, with no effort to rush.

She was the only one who paced herself, and he watched with a mixture of relief and admiration as she crossed. He hauled her in when she drew close enough, and she landed on her feet and quickly unwound the rope around her waist. Her blouse and skirt clung to her lean, slender body and outlined every curve and contour.

"I'll be going back over now," he said. "Undress, spread your clothes in the sun to dry, and stay in the trees. I may not be able to get back for a while. When I get to the other side, untie the rope around the tree and let it go. I'll haul it back."

Verna nodded and Rosalie still appeared chalk-white and spent, he saw, but Abby had already hurried into the trees.

Fargo took a length of rope, tied it around his waist, and secured it to the ropeline. He plunged into the water and began to pull himself back to the other shore. The angry river tore at him and his wrist and forearm still hurt, but compared to his first trip across, this time was almost a lark.

When he reached the shore he saw Miguel waiting, and the boy rushed forward to stretch out a hand. Fargo took it, pulled himself onto the dry land, and turned to peer across the river. He grasped the ropeline as Verna untied the other end. The line plunged into the river like an endless, thin snake, whipping and twisting, but he finally hauled it to his side of the shore and slowly curled it into shape to hang back on the saddle. He walked to the Ovaro, pulled a towel from his saddlebag, and dried himself thoroughly. When he finished, he dressed quickly and swung onto the horse.

"Get the jenny, Miguel," he said. "It's time for a leisurely ride downriver." Miguel pulled himself onto the mule and rode beside him as he moved out of the thicket and left the other three horses behind. He cut north first, moved out of the trees, and then, at a walk, rode east, now in clear sight of anyone along either riverbank.

Fargo made idle talk with Miguel as he rode into the open terrain where the river returned to its slow and sluggish self. When they reached the open shoreline, he spoke to the boy without looking at him. "Keep your eyes forward," he said. "Don't look across the river. We're not supposed to know they're back in those trees. When they come across after us, all you have to do is look surprised."

"*Sí*, I understand." Miguel nodded.

"We ought to be having company pretty damn soon now," Fargo murmured out of the side of his mouth. His prediction had only another few minutes to wait before it was fulfilled as the line of horsemen burst from the trees on the opposite bank and crossed the slow and sluggish river at a gallop. Fargo drew to a halt as Jim Halpin rode out of the water, the man's square-cut face darkened with a frown.

"Where are the girls?" he barked.

Fargo fastened a calm stare at him. "They left."

"What do you mean, they left? What are you trying to pull?" Halpin snapped.

"I'm not pulling anything, friend," Fargo said. "They decided to end their search. I guess you and the silver-mine bunch convinced them to forget the money."

"I don't believe they just up and quit after coming all this way."

"All I know is they paid me off and the boy decided to stay with me. I promised him I'd see him to the border," Fargo said. "They rode off together, headed straight north."

"Goddamn, I'm not letting them go off together just like that. I think they know more than they told you or anybody else." The Pinkerton man frowned.

Fargo shrugged. "I told them they ought to keep on looking, but they said no and told me I was through."

"Well, that was one goddamn quick about-face. I'm not falling for it," Halpin said, and backed his horse around the jenny. "Let's go," he said to his men. "I want to catch up to them before they decide to get real cute and split up."

"Hell, they may have done that already. They left me over an hour ago."

Halpin threw a curse into the wind and led his men off at a gallop.

Fargo held his smile back until they were out of sight.

"What about the other ones, from the silver-mine company?" Miguel asked.

"They'll sit at the other end of the river for a while longer, maybe another hour, until they decide something's wrong, and then they'll come chasing down to this end. They'll pick up the hoofprints of the Pinkerton boys racing north, figure they must be chasing the girls, and follow after them," Fargo said. "While the whole lot of them are back chasing their tails around north, we'll be on our way. Meanwhile, we'll stay out of sight in that thicket of shadbush." He moved toward the cluster of low, shrubby trees with Miguel following. They made their way out of sight in the foliage and dismounted.

Fargo estimated a little more than an hour had passed when he heard the sound of hoofbeats come down the shoreline and halt. Then he heard Sam Schreiber's commands and the hoofbeats sounded again. Fargo waited, let them disappear from hearing range, and moved out of the shrubby trees with Miguel. He rode back to where the river became a raging rapids, retrieved the three horses, and led them down to the calm waters at the other end. He crossed there, leading the three horses behind, Miguel at his side. Once on the opposite shore, he turned upriver and rode along the shoreline.

The river began to turn wild again, and soon he was alongside the foam-swept rapids and saw Verna step from the trees, still buttoning her blouse.

"You all dried out?" he asked.

"Dry enough," she said, and Rosalie came forward looking more herself than when he'd left her. Abby emerged last, tucking her blouse into her skirt.

"It worked," Fargo said. "They're all racing north after you. They'll probably spend at least three days trying to find you."

"Meanwhile?" Verna queried.

"We go west," Fargo said, and cast a glance at the sky. "It'll be dark in another hour or so. I'll find a place to camp and you can tell me what ideas you've come up with about those damn tattoos." He waited for the three young women to mount their horses and then set off at a fast canter, turned west, and made his way through the dry rock terrain.

It was near dusk when he found a small alcove of rock with some scrub brush, and he swung from the Ovaro, unsaddled the horse, and made a small fire. He felt the tiredness on him and saw the fatigue in Rosalie's face as she slid from her horse. It showed less in Verna and Abby, but it was there in the small tight lines that touched their mouths.

He heated some of the dried beef strips over the fire and the meal was quickly finished. He leaned back on one elbow in the last flickering light and scanned the three young women. "Who wants to go first?" he asked. An uneasy silence followed his question, and it was Rosalie who spoke first, anger and frustration in her voice.

"I haven't come up with anything more. I still say Tom Yancey meant that we have to work together to find it. He said that much in his note. We can't find it alone, he said."

"And I still say the tattoos are some kind of sign he gave each of us to find," Verna put in. "It might even be a roadside marker."

"What road? Where? You could wander a lifetime looking for that. If it's a sign, it has to mean more than that," Fargo said, and Verna's lips tightened glumly.

"Besides, if he gave us each the same sign to look for, why did his note say we couldn't find it alone?" Abby asked, and Verna shrugged and looked even more glum.

"We're all exhausted. Let's get some sleep and go at it again in the morning," Fargo said, and Rosalie nodded gratefully.

He took his bedroll up through a narrow passage in the rocks, walked over to a flat protrusion of rock, and set his things out. He undressed and lay down, too tired to pursue any ideas about tattoos and notes and cryptic meanings. He fell asleep quickly, and when dawn came, he rose and peered out over the dry terrain below. The Mexican border lay only a dozen miles to the south. This was all land where Tom Yancey had once been the scourge of whatever suited his fancy. The answer to the riddle he had left the three young women had to be out there in the red sandstone and scrubby shadbush. But without something more to go on, it would indeed be like looking for a needle in a haystack.

The damn tattoos, Fargo swore as he dressed. They had to hold the answer. The frown still creased his brow as he went down through the passage and found everyone up and ready to ride.

"Where to now?" Verna asked despondently.

"We have to find something more," Fargo said.

"I don't think there is anything more," Abby answered. "We have the answer. It's someplace in what he's given us. We just can't understand it."

"That's why we need something more to help us," Fargo said. "There's a tiny hovel of a town halfway to the border, not much more than a stopping place where a man can get water for his horse and whiskey for his throat. I'm damn sure Tom Yancey's been there often enough. Maybe somebody will tell us something, any little thing that might help us."

"It's worth a try. God knows I don't have any better ideas," Verna said.

"Then let's ride," Fargo said, and climbed onto the Ovaro.

Verna rode beside him, and Miguel rode a few paces back with Abby and Rosalie as the Trailsman wandered downward, found a dusty road, and took it south and west. It was noon when he found his way to the four, flat-roofed, whitewashed buildings, more Mexican in appearance than Yankee.

"This place have a name?" Verna asked.

"Polvo Caliente, a fitting name if I ever saw one," Fargo said, and Verna's glance questioned. "It means Hot Dust," he explained as they drew up before the largest of the four structures.

Two sleepy-eyed figures lounging against the outside wall near the door looked up from their wide-brimmed hats, and their eyes widened as they saw the three young women.

Fargo dismounted and Verna was the first to follow him into the building. It was a combination trading post and bar where a broad-faced, olive-skinned man lounged behind a short bar flanked by rows of blankets, hides, and sombreros. A heavy-busted woman with long black hair and a red shirt sat on the single bar stool. Sloe-eyed and coarse-featured, she eyed Verna, Rosalie, and Abby with more surprise than admiration.

*"Buenas tardes,"* the man said.

" 'Afternoon," Fargo answered.

The man's eyes lingered on Rosalie before returning to Fargo. "Some tequila for the ladies?" he asked with a wolfish smile.

"Nothing for them," Fargo said. "But I'll take some." The bartender's smile broadened and he poured a shot glass of the clear liquid. As he took a deep draw of the tequila, Fargo noticed another man lounging at a small round table in a corner of the room. Wearing a sombrero pushed back on his head, he looked on with obvious curiosity.

"We don't have too many visitors these days, especially none like this," the bartender said with another glance at the three young women.

"Not like the days when Tom Yancey used to stop by, eh?" Fargo said between sips of the tequila.

"Señor Yancey? You knew him, *señor*?" The barkeep asked, caution in his voice at once.

"Not me, but these young ladies were friends of his," Fargo said. "He come by this way often?"

"Often enough," the man said.

"The young ladies are thinking of writing a story about Yancey. They're trying to find out more about him, where he spent most of his time, places he visited," Fargo said. "He ever spend the night here?"

"*Sí,* very often," the man said.

"Just the night?" Fargo pressed.

"*Sí.* He would go his way in the morning," the barkeep said. "Even a young *señorita* I had here could not tempt him."

"Thanks for talking to us. You have anything to eat here?"

"Tortilla sandwiches," the man said.

"We'll take six with us," Fargo said, and turned to Verna. "Wait outside," he said, and she led Abby and Rosalie from the house. The woman helped the barkeep fix the tortillas, and when they were ready, Fargo had Miguel help take them outside while he paid.

"Where are you going, *señor?*" the barkeep asked. "There is not much to see and less to do in this country."

"We'll just wander around some, get an idea of what sort of place Tom Yancey lived in," Fargo said with deceptive casualness.

"Señor Yancey never lived around here," the man said. "He just passed through and sometimes did a little robbery."

"Whatever," Fargo said, nodded good-bye, and strolled outside where Miguel and the girls were busily devouring their tortillas.

"I felt as though I were in Mexico in that place," Verna said between bites.

"This was Mexico a little over ten years ago," Fargo reminded her. "Borders change, not people. Ride while you eat," he said, and pulled himself onto the pinto.

"We didn't find out anything," Rosalie said as they rode from the town at a walk.

"More than you think," Fargo said, and she frowned. "We know now that Yancey never spent more than a night in Polvo Caliente, and that tells us he rode hard to get someplace in this general region and needed a good night's sleep before starting back to his cabin. Not even a young *señorita* could tempt him to stay, you heard the man say. Yancey was a man with a purpose when he passed through here. No casual pleasure visits. That means he hid his money someplace not too damned far from here."

"How far is not too far?" Rosalie queried.

"Anywhere from a mile to ten miles in any direction," Fargo said, and heard Abby join in Rosalie's groan.

"Back to the needle in a haystack," Rosalie said, and gestured to the vast region of red-brown rock formations and sparse shrubbery.

The remark was too close to truth, Fargo realized as he swept the terrain with a long glance. "We'll ride for a few days, make a series of careful circles so we don't backtrack on ourselves. Maybe we'll get lucky," he said with more confidence than he felt. "We're in the right area." He finished the tortilla and Verna put the extra one in her bag while he rode ahead, halted at a conelike pinnacle of yellow stone, and waited for the others to catch up to him. "We've time for one circle before night," he said. "We'll start here and make our way back. Everybody ride twenty yards apart."

"What are we supposed to look for?" Verna asked.

"You think the tattoos mean a sign. Look for that," he told her. "Rosalie thinks he hid the money in some old mine. Look for any signs of diggings."

"What are you going to look for?" Abby asked.

"Tracks. Old ones, lapping over one another. A man makes a lot of trips to the same place, he's going to leave enough tracks. Maybe I can pick them up," Fargo said, and saw the expression of skepticism on Abby's face. "Spread out. We'll meet back here," he said, and took the outer perimeter of the imaginary circle.

He rode slowly, his eyes searching the land on both sides, and he found but a few old tracks of a single horse wandering through the passages. He spotted a dozen unshod Indian pony tracks, also old and crumpled at the edges. He finally returned back to the pinnacle. The dry dust of the terrain didn't allow tracks to remain deep and clear, he realized, and the possibility of picking up Yancey's tracks remained a slim hope.

Verna returned next with Miguel beside her, then Abby and finally Rosalie. Fargo saw the night sliding down over the rocks. He found a place to bed down where a half-circle of red cedar had offered some shade and had kept the ground moderately cool.

"I didn't see anything that looked like an old dig," Rosalie grumbled.

"And nothing that even resembled those tattoos," Verna said.

"Get some sleep," Fargo said. "We'll start fresh in the morning." He tossed a reassuring smile at them, which he didn't even accept himself, and took his bedroll up a gentle slope. He found a spot where three red cedars formed a triangle, and set his things down. He undressed, his gun belt at the edge of his bedroll, and lay back to stare up at the black velvet sky. He watched the moon move high to coat the land with a pale-silver brush and heard a red wolf howl in the distance. This was not a land for giving up anything, he realized. A hard, dry land, it defied one to exist on its harsh terms, and it offered none of its own secrets and none of anyone else's. But the Comanche and the Apache had learned how to use the land, as had the Navaho and before the Navaho, the Hopi, Zuni, and Maricopa.

In his own way, so had Tom Yancey, but something still didn't fit. Yancey had a strange sense of humor, no more clearly shown than in what he'd done with Verna, Rosalie, and Abby. But he had left them signs to find. They were hidden and disguised, but they were there. Even in the note he had given them some clues. He wouldn't have left them something that couldn't be done, a quest beyond finding. That kind of cruelty wasn't Tom Yancey. A needle in a pincushion, maybe, but not a haystack.

Fargo's thoughts broke off as he heard the scrape of footsteps moving up the slope. He saw the slender figure appear, find him in the pale moonlight, and come toward him. "More things you want to say?" he asked mildly.

"Yes," she said. "And maybe a little confessing." Abby knelt down on the bedroll beside him and he saw the wry smile come to her lips, and suddenly she seemed softer, more open. "I've given up thinking about the tattoos, the money, all of it. I don't think we can ever find it," she said.

"I wouldn't say that yet," Fargo told her.

She shrugged. "But I have been thinking about something," Abby said, and he lifted an eyebrow in question. "Thinking about what you said about my not being as honest as Verna and Rosalie."

"Didn't say that exactly," Fargo corrected. "I said your honesty didn't go as far as theirs. There's a difference."

"Maybe. But it all comes out the same, and I've not stopped thinking about that. Maybe we'll be going our own ways soon, as empty-handed as when we started," Abby said. "But you've done more for us than any of us could've hoped for. I think you deserve my honesty."

"Aren't you mixing things up again?" Fargo said, and she frowned at him.

"Honesty isn't for somebody else. Honesty is for yourself first," he said, and she stared back with her eyes wide, his words moving through her.

"Yes, of course," she said and her fingers curled around the top button of her blouse, pulled it open, then quickly went to the others. In moments the blouse lay beside her and Fargo took in the loveliness of her breasts, upturned, perfectly shaped cups, each tipped with a pink nipple on a slightly darker circle, breasts that fitted the long, lean contours of her torso. With a quick, lithe motion she slipped the skirt down and stood before him, narrow hips, a flat abdomen, and a small but thick black triangle, thin, yet well-shaped legs. She was a lean, tight beauty with a tensile excitement.

She came to him, dropped down on her knees in front of him again, but this time her arms went around his neck and she pressed the upturned breasts into his chest. Her lips found his, a little tentative, with shades of hesitant desire, and he pressed her mouth open and let his tongue find her. She shivered and her kiss turned full and open. He drew her gently onto her back and took in the lean loveliness of her, ran both hands slowly down her body, across the upturned breasts, down her torso, delicately kneading the tight flesh of her thighs.

"Oh, oh, my God," Abby moaned as he brought his lips to one sweet breast, caressed the tiny pink tip with his tongue, gently circled the areola, and gathered its smooth softness into his mouth. She moaned again and her torso turned, twisted, and her arms pressed his face harder into her breast. "Yes, oh, wonderful . . . oh, so good . . . so good," she murmured, words spoken on gasps of breath.

His hand slid downward, a slow, sensuous path across her flat abdomen, then paused at the tiny indentation of her midsection and lingered there as she moaned in delight. He felt her body grow taut as his hand moved down, found the thick black triangle, and slid through the soft-wire nap to press on the surprisingly large Venus mound. Then his hand crept lower. Her thin inner thighs were moist, a warm wonderful moistness that sent its own message of desire. His hand gently caressed their soft flesh, parting skin pressed against skin, and Abby moaned, a soft and almost despairing sound.

He found the glass-smooth lips, touched gently, and Abby's moan grew louder. Her hand came down, closed around his wrist, and held him there, refusing to let him move deeper. He halted, waited, then brought his lips to her breasts and felt her fingers open and draw back from his wrist. He slid his hand forward and she half-screamed. "Oh, God, oh, oh . . . ooooh," Abby cried out, and her lean body lifted, legs falling open as the narrow petals of a flower. He came half over her and his pulsating warmth pressed down over the black triangle, touching her skin with its throbbing heat.

"Jesus . . . eeeeee . . ." Abby shouted, and her taut, lean form twisted, rose, then drew back, but came forward again for him as a half-cry, half-laugh came from her lips. "Yes, yes, yes . . . oh, Fargo, yes . . . do it. Oh, God, do it," her words flung out with a kind of desperate desire.

He moved, lifted his hips, let his burgeoned wanting touch her warmth, paused, then rested. He let the touch of flesh on flesh send its waves of fervid wanting coursing through her, coursing through his own self, and he slid forward, down the lubricious funnel, and heard Abby scream out against his chest as he pulled him to her. He moved in her, slowly, to and fro, felt her thin thighs tighten against his hips, quiver, fall open, and then tighten again. Her hands had become little fists that pounded against his back as she surged with him, screamed out each time, surged again, and the lean desperate desire remained part of her. "Yes, yes . . . oh, yes, more, more," she murmured through gasped breaths, and he felt her grow more tense, her body trembling as she pushed with him, and the beautifully cupped breasts quivered, their little points standing firm.

Then suddenly, he felt her contractions around him, her thighs grow taut against him, becoming a vise of flesh and desire. Abby flung her head back as she began to gasp out short screams. "Ah . . . ah . . . now, now, I . . . I . . . I'm coming . . . oh, oh," she flung out, and her fists were pounding furiously against his back now. He let the pent-up hunger of his own explode with her, the ecstasy of time hanging in mid-air, the flesh reaching out and drawing in all in one moment of turbulent sensation. He heard his own groaned gasp of release as Abby suddenly fell limp with a cry of dismay wrapped in pleasure and the thin thighs fell from him. She lay with him, her breath made of thin gasps until finally she was able to draw a long sigh.

She half-turned against him, breasts a wondrously soft touch against his chest as he lay beside her. "The pleasures of honesty," she murmured.

"Sometimes pleasure, sometimes pain," he said. "But it's always best that way. You're not honest inside, you're not honest outside."

"It's been a long time for me, but I wasn't being dishonest. There was just never anyone that reached me . . . till you," Abby said.

"I'm glad," he murmured, and she rose on one elbow and began to pull her blouse on.

"The others were hard asleep when I left. I want to

get back before they wake up," Abby said. "This was between us. No one else has to know."

"No one," he agreed. He rose, and when she had her skirt on, he kissed her again, and there was no hesitancy in her lips.

"Maybe we'll find another time," she murmured.

"Maybe," he said, and watched her hurry into the darkness, a lean, slender figure still fashioned of contained propriety. But it could be uncontained . . . He smiled as he lay down. Very uncontained.

He slept at once, grateful for the power of honesty.

gested," Fargo said. "He wrote that line

# 7

Fargo woke with the dawn and scanned the terrain with its maze of rock formations. He felt the frustrated anger curling inside him as he became more certain that the answer was indeed under his nose, in the things Tom Yancey had done and said and written. When he finished washing with the water from his canteen, he dressed and hurried down to find the others awake and preparing to ride.

"Let me see that note again," he said to Verna, and she rummaged in her bag and pulled it out. He frowned as he read it over once, twice, and then a third time. His eyes had grown narrow in thought as he handed the note back to Verna and faced them. "I think we've been reading it wrong, especially that line about none of you being able to find it alone," he said. "He wrote that you have to be together, all three of you."

He watched them frown back, their eyes questioning. "Be together," Fargo said. "Not work together, not pool your brains or your muscles. Be together, each with your tattoos. If Abby hadn't been so proper, hers would be on her ass, too."

"But what's it mean? They're all alike," Rosalie said.

"Maybe they mean something if you put them together," Fargo said. "He wrote that if only one or two of you found the cabin, you wouldn't be able to find the money. Why? Because one or more of the tattoos would be missing." He turned, searched the ground for a moment, and found a short piece of shrub branch with one end pointed enough. "Lay down, on your stomachs and let me see your tattoos."

Rosalie started to stretch herself prone and Verna halted halfway to the ground. "Not with Miguel looking on. He's just a boy yet," she said.

"I'll look away, Verna," Miguel said quickly, and Fargo held the smile inside himself.

"You heard the boy," he barked. "Let's see those tattoos. You lie next to them, Abby, so I can see the back of your knee alongside the others." He waited, watched Rosalie lie prone and lift her skirt up, saw Verna do the same and Abby turn the back of her knee to him. He peered at the tattoos and tried not to be distracted by the lovely, round rears. He took the stick and drew the first tattoo on the loose trail dust in the ground, copying it exactly. He moved, drew Verna's tattoo in dust alongside Rosalie's, and finished with Abby's.

"All right, ladies, that's it. Don't let the sun burn your fannies." He shot a glance at Miguel, who stood with his face averted. "You can look now, Miguel," he said.

Abby was the first to come alongside him and peer down at the three tattoos he had drawn side by side in the dust. "They don't mean any more to me together than they did separately," she murmured.

"Me neither," Rosalie chimed in.

"Same here," Verna agreed, and Fargo stared with them in silence, unable to find any answer either. It was Miguel's voice that broke into the silence, a soft gasp, first, then a shout.

"*Caramba!* Los Tres Hermanos," the boy bit out.

"The three brothers?" Fargo echoed.

"*Sí*, three peaks, right on the border west of Pancho Villa," Miguel said. "They stand together, exactly the same height. Los Tres Hermanos, they have always been called that in Mexico. At the bottom, in front of them, is a long row of stone cliff houses, the kind used by the Pueblo long ago."

Fargo brought his eyes back to the drawing in the dust. "The little squares at the bottom," he breathed. "Put together like this they run along the bottom of the three peaks. By God, that's it."

"Yes, that's it," Verna chortled. "Jesus, that's it, all right."

"He put one peak on each of you, and the little squares for the cliff houses below it. That's why you had to be together. Only then could you put all three peaks together," Fargo said.

"He wanted all three of us to share the money," Verna said soberly. "All three, or none of us."

"Damn his weird ways," Rosalie said. "We'd never have figured it out alone."

"You might have. Maybe it'd have taken you longer, but you might have," Fargo said.

"Maybe. A big maybe," Abby said. "But he did play fair with us, in his own crazy way."

"Tom Yancey was one of a kind, that's for sure," Fargo said, and used his foot to wipe out the drawing in the dust. He finished and saw Verna hugging Miguel to her. "Let's ride. We have to pay a visit to three brothers," Fargo said and watched everyone almost leap onto their mounts.

Miguel rode beside him as he turned south toward the border. The sky suddenly turned dark and stormy ahead of them and he saw flashes of lightning. "Want to camp out someplace?" he asked, and received a chorus of nos and glanced at Miguel.

"We might reach the Three Brothers before the storm." The boy shrugged. "It is only a few hours' ride."

"Let's try," Fargo said, and put the pinto into a fast canter.

The storm was off to the east, still swirling around itself but not moving very much, he saw, undoubtedly trapped in a pocket it had created itself. He swung the horse westward while still heading south, and as was the way of the dry, semidesert New Mexico land, while the distant storm poured watery fury in one place, the sun burned in another. He finally called a halt after another hour as he saw the horses panting hard. "They need a rest," he said to Verna, Rosalie, and Abby. "So do you, only you're all too excited to know it."

They slid to the ground and he saw the relief in their faces as they sat down. "I'm a little hungry. The extra tortilla is in my bag. We can all have a little," Rosalie said.

"You three split it. I've enough beef strips for Miguel and myself," Fargo said, and sat down to have a late and sparse lunch.

"I just had a terrible thought," Verna remarked. "What if the money's not there? Or what if we can't find it after we get there?"

"If it's there, we'll find it," Rosalie said with grim determination. "And it's got to be there."

Verna shrugged. "Maybe not. Tom Yancey had his strange ways. Fargo said it when we first started. Maybe this is just one last joke on his part," she countered.

"No," Fargo cut in. "I thought that once, but not anymore. That wouldn't fit the man's character. That'd be cruel, and I've seen or heard nothing of cruelty in Yancey's ways." He pushed to his feet, his gaze traveling down the horizon at the distant purple-black turbulence. "Let's ride," he said. "That storm's moving, but it doesn't seem to know which way it wants to go." He slid into the saddle and led the way west, then south again. They had gone another hour when a high wall of red rock rose up to blot out the view, and he spurred the Ovaro into a gallop until he was past the obstacle. He reined to a halt and peered into the distance.

Verna was first to reach him, and Miguel next as the boy rode the jenny hard. Fargo saw Verna follow his gaze to where the three tall peaks rose up, side by side, in the distance. "The Three Brothers," she gasped.

"*Sí, sí,*" Miguel said. "Los Tres Hermanos. They look the same from this side of the border."

Fargo felt a gust of hot wind blow against his face and turned to peer east at the storm. It was still far away, but it seemed to be moving toward them now, gathering direction and momentum. A powerful thunderstorm in this dry country, fed by the spirals of winds it created, could move with fearful speed and spawn its own series of tornadoes.

Fargo motioned to the others and put the pinto into a gallop as he set out across the uneven terrain toward the three peaks. He was three-quarters of the way toward his goal when the wind began to swirl around him. He glanced back to see the purple-black turbulence rushing toward him, not unlike a giant vulture that suddenly spotted its prey. He continued to ride hard, rounded a low row of sandstone formations, and reined to a halt as the three peaks rose up in front of him.

He heard the gasps of anticipation as the girls halted beside him, but his eyes were sweeping the rows of almost square openings that ran along the base of the peaks, the cliff houses of a people that once pioneered agriculture in this dry land as they fashioned homes out of the forbidding rock. "Tattoos become reality," he said to Abby, who moved alongside him. But a grimace touched his lips as he swept the cliff houses again. "Yancey tattooed four squares on each of you, four under each peak. I count at least twenty-four cliff houses, not twelve," he said.

"The tattoos were a guide, not a map," Abby said. "Which means we'll have to search each of them."

The gust of wind that slammed into Fargo's back had sudden power to it, and he turned in the saddle to see the sky had become an overpowering, menacing expanse of purple and gray. He caught the spiral funnel gathering itself at one side of the storm, whipping itself into winds that would quickly be beyond measure, winds that could kill with shredding, whirling force.

"Ride," he barked, and sent the pinto racing for the first and nearest of the cliff-house openings. The ground rose up toward the cliff dwellings, which sat on higher land, and he found a wide pathway and sent the pinto up it in a full gallop. He pulled to a halt at the entrance to the first of the cliff houses and was grateful to see it was high enough to bring the horses inside.

He dismounted and pulled the Ovaro behind him as he stepped into the rock-lined, cavelike space and saw it was deep enough to hold everyone. A hissing sound swirled from outside and he saw Verna come in first, leading her horse, then Miguel, pulling the jenny along with him. Abby and Rosalie entered next, just as a tremendous thunderclap resounded. Almost instantly, the rain slammed into the rock that formed the roof of the dwelling, and the tremendous winds hissed outside.

Fargo knelt on one knee and his lips pulled back as he heard the hissing roar that signaled a twister spiraling its way across the land.

"We're lucky," he said. "If we'd been caught outside, it might've meant the end of your search."

"How long will it last?" Rosalie asked.

"The twister will move on. The rain and high winds could last an hour or a day."

"It's not bad in here. Plenty of air, especially with more being blown in," Verna said.

"But there's nothing in here but us," Abby pointed out.

"I expect they'll all be that way, except for one," Fargo said as he lowered himself to the stone floor and leaned back against one of the walls. He cast a glance outside where the dark turbulence and driving rain was a curtain of fury. "Even if this storm only lasts another hour, it'll be too late to start exploring. It'll be night by then, so you can prepare to bed down in here," he said.

"I've been in worse hotels," Rosalie said.

Fargo rose, set out his bedroll, and handed an extra blanket to Abby. "One of you still has my other blanket and one of you can use my rain slicker." He took off his shirt as night fell, and he lay down, listening to the others settle themselves.

Outside, the storm continued to fill the night with its windswept rain, and Fargo stretched out, closed his eyes, and was almost asleep when he felt the warm, naked body against him. He stayed motionless for a long moment, then slowly moved his hand down along the smooth, soft skin, tracing the contours of the back, waist, rear.

"Good night, Abby," he whispered, and felt the form snuggle in closer to him. He smiled and was glad for an educated touch as he let sleep come to him. The steady rain formed a kind of lullaby and the storm lasted most of the night.

When he woke as the gray of dawn began to seep into the cliff house, he noticed the silence outside. Abby lay beside him, her lean nakedness lovely in the half-light. He rose, pulled on his shirt, and she stirred and woke to see him go to the entrance of the dwelling. The sun was beginning to appear over the distant rocks and his eyes swept the terrain just below the dwellings. The wind and rain had washed rock silt down in a layer. It would quickly become one more layer of earth in the dry terrain. That was the way of this land, forever draining, yet adding to itself through the action of wind and rain, the seemingly changeless forever changing. But the ancient Pueblo had known this, had used it in their lives, and had built their cliff dwellings safe from the unpredictability of nature.

He turned back into the cave and saw Abby dressed, the others awake and pulling on clothes. Miguel finally pulled his eyes open and sat up. "Don't hurry," Fargo told them. "We'll be here until noon, I'd guess. We have to give the sun time to dry out the rock silt or you and the horses will break your legs slipping and sliding."

Disappointment flooding each of their faces, they hurried to the entranceway to stare down.

"It looks firm enough to me," Rosalie said. "All we have to do is go down and cross to the next cave."

"That's right. It seems simple, but it's impossible," Fargo said. "Sit down and wait." He peered outside to where the sun was beginning to stretch across the land. "Noon," he grunted.

"You're being too damn cautious," Rosalie flared. "I haven't come this far to sit around twiddling my thumbs. I'm going to start looking for that money." She glared at Verna and Abby, waited for their support, and received only uncertain glances. "I'll be waiting for you with the money," she snapped, and stalked from the house.

Fargo watched from the entranceway, Verna and Abby standing beside him as Rosalie started down the wide path on foot. She had taken a few dozen steps when her feet went out from under her and she fell on her ample rump and slid to the bottom.

"Damn," she swore when she came to a stop, and he watched her try to pull herself up. The rock silt slid from under her and she went down, on her stomach this time. She tried to push to her feet again and the earth slid away beneath her and she sprawled, slid a half-dozen feet, and came to rest against a protruding piece of rock. Once again she tried to regain her feet only to fall. Fargo saw her look up to where he watched, her silt-covered breasts heaving with deep breaths. "Throw me a rope, dammit," she called.

"The sun will dry it all out, you with it now," Fargo called back.

"Damn you, Fargo," she screamed.

"Relax," he said, and turned back into the cavernous cliff house.

"Will she be all right?" Abby asked.

"She'll be fine," he said, and lowered himself to his bedroll. "Relax," he muttered, and closed his eyes. He napped on and off and finally rose after the sun had grown hot again. He went to the entranceway to see Abby slowly pulling herself to her feet. He returned into the cave and gathered up his bedroll as the others pulled their gear together. "Lead your horses," he said as he left the cave with the pinto. "One of you bring Rosalie's mount."

He went outside, carefully tested the new layer of ground, and found the sun had quickly begun its work of creating another layer of sediment that would soon become the hard, dry dust of the land. He led the way down to where Rosalie glared at him, and Verna brought her horse to her.

"You start. I'll change and clean up and catch up to you," Rosalie said with a glower, and Fargo moved past her to where the next entranceway beckoned. He left the Ovaro and hurried inside, Verna and Abby close behind him. The space was almost as large as the other and just as empty, though he took the time to explore to the back of it.

Rosalie was with them by the time they climbed to the next cave and found it not quite as empty, a scattering of dry branches across the stone floor. But nothing else was there, and they went on to the next one, moving the horses with them each time. Some of the cliff dwellings were smaller than others, some were mustier, a few had broken shards of stone pottery along the walls, and some had alcoves at the back that took extra time to explore.

They had gone through three-quarters of the stone dwelling places and found more with half-burned wood where fires had been made not more than months back. "Maybe someone was here, came onto the money by accident, and took it," Rosalie muttered. "The remains of these fires show that somebody was here."

"I'd guess these were ritual fires made by the Navaho," Fargo said. "They use these old Pueblo dwellings for their own rituals."

Rosalie allowed hope to touch her face and followed him outside to the next cave. But he halted, stepped back, and surveyed the line of cliff dwellings they had so far explored. They had all been empty, but he frowned as he began to count from the other end, where they had still to explore. "Four squares on each tattoo," he murmured. "Twelve altogether. We try that one," he said, and pointed to an entranceway a few yards down. "That's the twelfth one from the end, we haven't explored it yet."

He led the way into the cliff house and saw it was one of those with an alcove at the rear. Abby was beside him when he turned into the alcove and he heard her gasp of excitement. Some ten sacks and an old tin box lined the rear wall, and Abby's eyes turned to him.

"Bull's-eye," he said, grinning and she let out a scream of delight that was instantly echoed by Rosalie and Verna. They pushed past him and fell upon the sacks, yanking open drawstrings, spilling coins and paper currency onto the floor.

"We found it, we found it," Rosalie shouted as she tossed a handful of coins into the air.

Fargo let them open each sack, some holding only a few coins, others heavy with money. As Abby opened the last sack, he strode to the tin box, pulled the latch up, and lifted the lid to stare down at the contents.

"I'll be damned!" He smiled. "Look at this."

The others gathered around at once as he lifted a small bundle of tubular objects tied together. "Dynamite," he said. "Tom Yancey probably grabbed it in one of his holdups and just put it here with the rest of his loot."

"We can leave that," Abby said firmly, and returned to the pile of coins that now formed their own pyramid on the stone floor.

"Start dividing it," Fargo said, and Verna nodded as she sat down in front of the pile of coins and stacked the currency. Rosalie and Abby lowered themselves beside her and Fargo leaned back as the three young women carefully began to divide the money. They had nearly finished, a task that took a lot longer than they'd expected, when Fargo heard the Ovaro snort in alarm and felt the tension seize his every muscle at once. He saw the girls push to their feet to hurry after him. They were at his heels when he reached the entrance to the cave and stepped outside. He stared at the two rows of uniformed soldiers lined up outside the cliff dwelling, each astride a light-boned black horse, each wearing the black, green, and gold trim of the Mexican army.

An officer with captain's bars on the shoulders of his uniform moved his horse forward. A trim, slender figure with a pencil-thin mustache, the man offered a smile. "*Buenas tardes*. I am Captain Santos López of the First Mexican Cavalry," he said.

Fargo felt the ice sliding through him and he silently swore at Tom Yancey. But he nodded to the officer, moved down to the Ovaro, and led the horse back to the entrance of the cliff dwelling before he turned to face the Mexican again. "You lost, Captain?" he asked.

"Lost?" The Mexican officer frowned. "Why do you ask that, *señor*?"

"Because you're on American soil," Fargo said.

"Only a half-mile." Captain Santos López smiled.

"Half-mile, ten miles, what's the difference," Fargo said. "You're not supposed to be here. If a troop of U.S. soldiers sees you, it could mean a lot of trouble."

"I'll say it was an accident. The border is hardly well-marked," the officer said. "Besides, my sentries have told me there is no one here but us."

"Meaning what exactly?" Fargo asked even as he knew the answer.

"Meaning that the money these charming *señoritas* have found belongs to the Mexican government," the captain said. "Señor Yancey enjoyed crossing the border to rob our payroll couriers. He was very clever, and we could never catch him. He had a different approach each time."

"So what makes you think we know anything about that money?" Fargo asked.

Captain Santos López smiled chidingly. "We too heard how Yancey died at a doctor's office and were told how he had left the money to three *señoritas*. We always suspected he hid his money somewhere in this region. We offered a sizable reward for any information about anyone new in the area, especially three *señoritas*. You made the mistake of stopping at Polvo Caliente and then talking about Yancey."

"The barkeep told you," Fargo said grimly.

"Of course. We had only to pick up your tracks. It wasn't difficult," the man said. "Now, we'll take the money and you can go on your way."

"You'll take nothing," Fargo snapped. "You're on American soil. You're not supposed to be here, and you're not taking anything."

He saw the officer's brows lift in mild reproof. The man half-turned in the saddle and swept his troops with a glance, then brought his eyes back to Fargo. "You have trouble seeing, *señor*?" he slid out. "You have three *señoritas* and a boy. I have a full squad of cavalry. I do not think you have a choice."

"I think different," Fargo growled.

The Mexican smiled again, tolerant amusement in his disdain. "You seem like a man who could play your American game of poker," he said. "I learned to play when I was a prisoner during the war. A fine game. I learned to like it very much. You have a losing hand, my friend. You have three queens. I have a full house."

Fargo cursed inwardly, but his chiseled face showed no emotion. "I'll play my hand," he said.

"You can't win. You know three queens can't beat a full house, *señor*." The captain smiled. He glanced at the sky where the long shadows of dusk had begun to slide across the rock formations. "I understand a good bluff. Every good poker player knows the value of a good bluff. But a good player also knows when he can't win. I will give you until tomorrow morning to throw in your hand. You have come a long way and it is hard to lose. But you can't win."

Fargo turned to Verna and Rosalie. "Bring the horses up," he muttered, then waited as they did. Miguel pulled the mule along behind them. "Everybody inside," he growled, and waited for them to disappear inside the cliff house before he turned back to the captain.

"Till tomorrow morning," the officer said. "Don't try to sneak out, *señor*."

"Wouldn't think of it," Fargo answered, turned his back on the soldiers, and strode into the cavern dwelling, where Verna, Abby, and Rosalie stared at him with dejection and defeat.

"Damn, damn, damn," Verna said. "All this way for nothing."

"Finish dividing up the money before it gets too dark in here," Fargo said, and saw their incredulous glances.

"Why? What difference does it make now?" Verna asked.

"There won't be time for counting, come morning," Fargo said.

"Are you crazy? You can't fight off the Mexican army," Rosalie snapped. "We've run out of time and tricks."

"Not yet," Fargo said. "You can thank Tom Yancey again." As they watched, he strode to the alcove of the dwelling and took out the dynamite sticks. "One of these can take care of ten of his men. He has some forty soldiers by my quick count. Now hurry up and finish dividing the money. I'll tell you the rest of the plan later.''

Abby was the first to return to the coins, and by the time dark came to turn the cave into a stygian hole, they had everything divided, each with their share in their sacks.

Fargo strode to the entranceway, Verna and Abby beside him. The pale moonlight showed that the captain had spread his men in a half-circle in front of the entrance, sentries posted every six feet. Fargo moved back into the blackness and felt more than saw the three figures gathered around him. "Come morning, I'm going to show the captain how a good poker player always has a hole card ready," he said. "When I start tossing dynamite, you four race your horses out of here, turn, and stay alongside the cliff-house line. You ride hard and ride north. Santos López won't have many men left to chase you, and more important, he won't dare chase you very far. He's over the border too far now and he knows it. He can't risk causing an incident that'll go far beyond the damn money. Everybody understand?"

*"Sí,"* Miguel said, and the others murmured agreement.

"Get some sleep, get as much as you can," Fargo said as he lay down, put his hands behind his neck, and closed his eyes.

He managed to sleep some, and woke with the first dawn light that slid its way into the cliff house. He saw Abby sit up and the others come awake quickly. "Mount up," he said. "Then stay back and wait for my orders." He started past Abby when her hand caught his arm.

"What happens to you?" she asked, her eyes deep with concern.

"I catch up to you later, if I'm lucky." He grinned

and hurried back to the dynamite. He untied the individual sticks, brushed the fuses with his fingers, and set the explosives down at the edge of the entranceway as he stepped outside. The captain had his troops mounted, lined up in threes just outside the entrance.

"Time to play poker," Fargo said, and the Mexican frowned.

"Ridiculous," the captain snapped. "Three queens cannot beat a full house."

"Three queens high bid. Call me," Fargo snapped, and saw the captain's face darken with anger. The man whirled in the saddle and barked at his troops.

"Attack," he shouted, and Fargo saw the horses quickly go into a full charge. He stepped back from the mouth of the cliff house and lighted two of the dynamite sticks as a half-dozen rifle bullets slammed into the stone. He counted off another five seconds, saw the dry fuses burning fast, and tossed both sticks out at the charging troopers that rode directly at the entranceway. He had the next two sticks lighted before the first two exploded, and he heard the screams of pain and surprise. He threw the next two, one more to the right this time, the other to the left.

The second round of explosions brought another set of screams and curses. Fargo tossed still two more dynamite sticks, but now he rose and ran to the front of the entranceway. The captain's men were in disarray, most littering the ground, and he spied the officer to one side as he tried to rally the last ten of his men. Fargo spun on his heels. "Get out of here now," he shouted. "Fast and hard."

Verna was the first out and he saw her wheel her horse north the minute she cleared the cave. Rosalie and Abby followed at her heels, with Miguel trailing on the mule.

"After them," Fargo heard the captain shout, and

saw him wheel his mount around. Fargo vaulted onto the Ovaro, lighted the last of the dynamite sticks, and raced from the cliff house. He charged straight down, tossed the dynamite in a wide, high arc, and saw it explode just over the last set of troopers. The uniformed figures flew from their mounts in all directions.

Fargo whirled to see the captain racing at him, a carbine raised. But the man fired too quickly, anger and haste destroying his aim. Fargo ducked, drew the Colt, and fired two shots at the onrushing rider. The first hit the captain in the arm, the second plowed into his shoulder. The carbine fell from the officer's hands as he toppled from his horse and lay on the ground, pushing himself to one knee, his face contorted in pain.

"Three queens don't beat a full house," Fargo said. "But four queens do, especially if one of them is dynamite." He turned the Ovaro, paused again to see the man staring after him, holding his shoulder with his other hand. "One more lesson. Never be sure a man's bluffing," Fargo said, and sent the pinto into a gallop. He cast a glance back at the scene. Some of the soldiers were beginning to pick themselves up, victims more of shock than anything else. But the captain wouldn't be taking them anywhere but back across the border, a short limp home. Fargo kept the pinto racing north until he came in sight of Miguel on the jenny.

The boy heard him, looked back, and shouted as he pulled the mule to a halt. Abby was first to come back to where Miguel had stopped, and Verna and Rosalie came soon after. Fargo tossed a grin at them. "It's over," he said. "You're home free."

"Oh, God," Verna breathed. "I'd given up hope of seeing this day."

"You wouldn't have seen it except for Fargo. None of us would," Abby said.

"Amen to that," Verna said, and moved her horse forward, leaned from the saddle, and embraced the big man on the Ovaro. Rosalie followed her and then Abby leaned her lips over to his.

"I hate to say it, but how do we get back through this dry, wild, Comanche-filled country?" Rosalie asked.

"I'll take you to Las Cruces. They've a good, reliable stage there that goes east in short hops with plenty of men riding shotgun," Fargo said, and Rosalie nodded happily.

The trip to Las Cruces was made even shorter by the coins each carried, and when they reached the town, the stage was there and taking on passengers. Rosalie and Verna sold their horses and saddles to the owner of the general store and bought their stage tickets when they returned. Abby remained on her horse and Fargo cast her a curious glance as Verna and Rosalie halted before him.

"We feel we ought to give you some of the money, Fargo. We wouldn't have it if it weren't for you," Verna said.

"You paid me. That was the deal and it'll stay that way," Fargo said. "But you each owe me your share for Otis Frawley's herd. I'll be getting that to him soon as I get back."

"Yes, of course," Verna said sheepishly, and fished the money from her sack.

Rosalie did the same and handed him her share. "Still not admitting anything," she murmured.

"Naturally," Fargo said. "I'll tell Otis it's out of the kindness of your hearts." He put the money into a leather purse in his saddlebag and turned to the two young women again. "What are you going to do with all you have left?"

"Miguel and I are going to enjoy life, maybe buy a little place somewhere," Verna said as the boy clung to her.

"I'm going to buy my own dance hall," Rosalie said.

He turned to Abby. "Put it away, a nest egg," she said.

"Why are you still sitting in that saddle?" He frowned.

"Because I'm not going on the stage," Abby said. "I'm riding with you."

"Just like that?" he remarked.

"Just like that. Honesty, it's called," she said.

"Why not?" He smiled and watched Verna, Miguel, and Rosalie climb aboard the stage. He waited, watched it roll away, and then he pulled himself onto the Ovaro and rode from town with Abby beside him.

He had reached the flat land north of Las Cruces when he saw Abby had pulled to a halt a half-dozen yards behind him. He rode back to her. She was waving one hand out at the rocky-ribbed formations in the distance. "What are you doing?" he asked.

"Saying good-bye to Tom Yancey," she answered.

He felt the smile slide over his face. "Why not?" he muttered, and added his wave to hers.

**LOOKING FORWARD!**
The following is the opening
section from the next novel in the exciting
*Trailsman* series from Signet:

**THE TRAILSMAN #98**
**DESERT DESPERADOES**

*July, 1860, on the scorching
New Mexico Territory desert,
where beautiful women and death
lurk in the dusty shadows . . .*

The big man astride the magnificent black and white
pinto had Miss Candy on his mind when the stallion's
ears came to attention. The movement broke Skye
Fargo's reverie of the saucy, voluptuous woman far
behind him in Colorado.

He glanced down and somewhat to the right of the
Ovaro's head. A mouse darted from a clump of the
dry desert grass that dotted the desolate landscape.
When it was close to another clump, the mouse halted.
The powerful Ovaro's muscles tensed the instant it
heard the buzz of vibrating rattles start.

Of its own accord the pinto angled left and gave the coiled rattlesnake and its nocturnal victim extra space.

Unperturbed by the death scene playing out on the sand, Fargo looked at the lowering full moon and the constellations long familiar to him. He heard the mouse begin a squeak that ended abruptly; the diamondback had claimed a meal.

Fargo's gaze shifted to stare across the endless dim bronze desert floor in this part of the New Mexico Territory. He wanted to complete his journey south before falling victim to another blistering high noon. But he held back the urge to change the stallion's walk to a faster gait and rode on toward the invisible southern horizon.

Moments later, he noticed something looming ahead in the distance. Squinting and focusing his lake-blue eyes on the indistinct form, he spurred the pinto to trot.

Drawing closer, he made out the unmistakable outlines of several Conestogas parked in a defensive circle.

Approaching the moon-bathed wagons, he shouted, "Rider coming in!" so a sentry wouldn't mistake him for an Apache and start shooting.

Nobody fired at him. Neither did anyone call back.

Fargo rode to the nearest Conestoga, reined the big Ovaro to a halt, and peered through the back canvas drawn and secured for the night. He could just make out the dark forms of two people on a makeshift bed. "Anybody home?" he queried. He slapped the wagon with his palm. Neither person moved.

Knowing what he would find, he dismounted and climbed inside. He rolled the man over. A bullet hole in the man's forehead stared at him. Fargo didn't bother to check the woman clad in her nightdress.

He crawled through the wagon and dropped to the sand. Going to the next wagon he spotted the teams of mules and horses tethered to stakes a short distance to his left. That told him this massacre had not been the work of the Apaches, who preferred mule meat over all other kinds.

Inside the wagon, he found two adults and a child lying askew on the floorboards. Now he knew the massacre had happened so fast and had been carried out so efficiently that nobody had been able to grab a weapon, much less flee in the night.

He went to another wagon and looked in. A man lay naked on the bedding. His fancy top hat, which seemed a bit out of place in this setting, sat on the floorboards nearby, as though handy for donning the moment he awakened, which he'd never do. The weapon that fired the bullet had been held so close that it left powder burns between the man's eyes.

Fargo checked all of the wagons for a sign of life, but he found everyone dead. They hadn't been dead for long. In two instances he felt blood that wasn't yet congealed around the bullet holes in the men's chests.

He stepped to their camp fire, where a few embers still glowed. His hand touched the large coffeepot hanging from a strand of heavy wire above the fire. The pot felt lukewarm.

Fargo stood and went to the tethered animals and set them free. If they're lucky and don't hang around, he thought, they'd go straight to the nearest supply of water, something Fargo could use himself.

Returning to the wagons, he whistled for the pinto. He removed the lid from a water keg and let the Ovaro drink from it while he drank from another barrel and filled his canteen.

After quenching his thirst, he rummaged about in the wagons until he found food supplies. Fargo feasted on day-old biscuits and strips of dried beef. Back on the ground, he went to the wagon bearing hay and oats and took some of both to his stallion.

While he lingered, the moon went down. Shortly after its disappearance the less brilliant stars began to fade. He mounted up and rode with the morning star on his left.

Soon the sun, huge and red-orange, seemed to burst over the eastern horizon. Majestic and mighty though it appeared, Fargo wished it'd waited another hour before beaming down on him and the pinto. The cool desert night would quickly transform into unbridled, searing heat. For that reason he had opted to ride all night.

By the time the fiery orb inched halfway up into the sky, he had noticed a column of wispy black smoke on the southern horizon. He urged the Ovaro to canter and headed straight toward the smoke. Fargo knew it came from his destination, the village of Domingo. "What next?" he muttered.

A lone buzzard came literally out of nowhere. It made a wide, lazy circle high above the pinto, then flew north. Fargo muttered to himself. "Looks like the scavengers have picked up the scent of death."

As he rode toward the black smoke, he watched its ominous column bend abruptly and spread to the southwest, obviously caught in a current of fast-moving air. He rode on.

Nearing the border village—some said it was on the U.S. side, others claimed Mexico, and a few had it straddling the line—he noticed peasants laboring in the sun. As he rode closer, he saw they were busy digging graves. He counted nine already open and waiting. At least ten more were being dug. Passing through the graveyard, he spied a large red olla. A watery gleam covered the exterior. He turned the Ovaro to it and looked inside. Dismounting, he smiled. Fargo cupped his hands and dipped them into the tepid water, then held it to the Ovaro's waiting lips. After quenching the horse's thirst, he gulped several handfuls down his own sun-parched throat.

He mounted again and headed for the opening in the adobe wall that surrounded the village proper. The smoke rose somewhere close behind the old mission.

A funeral procession arrived at the opening at the same time Fargo did. He moved the Ovaro out of the way and stopped to watch the somber passage.

A boy, no more than twelve years old, led the procession. He looked down while slowly swinging a silver censer of smoldering incense on the end of a long silver chain. Behind the boy walked a short, slim priest who wore eyeglasses. The man's skin was a shade lighter than milk-white, in stark contrast to his black robe, the hem of which swept the ground. Fargo began to frown when he noticed the man wore scuffed cowboy boots. The frown deepened when he saw the priest's fingers were busy, working rather clumsily through the much-used long strand of dark wooden rosary beads he held. Neither the boy nor the priest glanced at Fargo.

Four men bearing the first wood coffin on their shoulders followed the priest through the gateway. Behind them came other men bearing eight more identical coffins. A crowd of black-veiled mourners brought up the rear of the procession.

A shot rang out.

The burial party halted. Before anyone could turn to look around, the air erupted with fierce Apache war cries.

Carbines barked.

Mourners broke ranks and ran for safety inside the wall. The coffins were quickly lowered to the ground. With fear in their eyes, the pallbearers fled through the opening and scattered, each seeking his own safety.

The terrified screams of the women could be heard over the loud war cries.

Fargo drew his Sharps from its saddle case, spurred the Ovaro through the crowded entrance, and raced to engage the savages.

The narrow dirt street met another, and Fargo swerved left. He then came to an abrupt right turn, took it, and blasted out of the labyrinth into the square. There he reined back hard. The pinto skidded to a halt.

Half-naked Apaches raced helter-skelter onto the square from its far side. Villagers ran before them, screaming, making it virtually impossible for Fargo to shoot.

He charged forward, riding straight for the attackers. He drew his Colt, shot one point-blank, wheeled around, and shot two more.

An Apache caught a woman from behind, threw her to the ground, and raised his tomahawk. Fargo shot him dead.

Four screaming Apaches rushed him. In quick order the Colt dropped three. He bloodied the fourth man's head with the Sharps' barrel, then paused to reload both weapons. As he did, two Apaches appeared on a rooftop to his left. Fargo shifted in the saddle and shot both with his Colt.

Most of the villagers' screams came from the south part of the hamlet. Fargo replaced the spent bullets in the Colt, then spurred the Ovaro to attack.

As he tore down a narrow dirt street and took a sharp left turn, the screams grew louder. Before him three Apaches held two of the village women captive. Fargo shot two of the savages as he raced in on them, then leaped from the saddle, and engulfed the third Apache in his arms. On the ground he shot the savage in the heart, then ran toward the next set of terrified screams.

An Apache stood on a roof and aimed his carbine at Fargo. Fargo spun out of the way and fired. Hurtling backward with a bloodstain on his naked chest, the Apache pulled the trigger. The bullet thudded into the adobe wall next to Fargo.

Fargo whistled for the Ovaro, mounted up, and reloaded while looking for red targets. Stalking now, he walked the horse up and down the narrow streets, watching the roof lines and glancing behind him now and then. He noted the smoke that came from a wood structure which he presumed was the community storehouse for corn.

The screams had slackened. He believed the Apaches had retreated until a shot was fired and a puff of dirt sprang up in front of the ovaro.

He glanced up, spotted the half-naked rifleman on a roof, and killed the Apache with one shot.

A peasant ran around the far corner, saw Fargo, stumbled, and fell. Fargo rode to him and told the terrified man to get up and get off the street.

Seeing no more of the savages, Fargo turned the Ovaro and threaded his way through the labyrinth back to the square.

One of the villagers cowered behind the well in the middle of the square. Fargo shouted to him, "Amigo, go up in the bell tower and look around! Tell me if you see any Apaches!"

The scared man shook his head. Fargo shouted angrily, "Goddammit, I said go!" The fellow jumped as though prodded and ran to the tower. While the frightened little man was getting in position, Fargo glanced about the area. The crumpled bodies of white clad villagers and half-naked Apaches were everywhere he looked. Lining the wall on the shady side of the mission were wounded men and women. Too many, too fast, he thought, from this fight. At least a dozen newly made wood coffins lay on the ground at the steps of the mission.

"Senor," the man in the bell tower shouted, "the Apaches are running away!" He pointed northeast.

"Good," Fargo muttered. In a loud voice he said, "All right, you people can come out now. It's safe. The Apaches have left."

A few people appeared at the corners of the streets to peer around them and make sure it was safe before they ventured out into the open plaza and fully exposed themselves. Fargo turned the Ovaro and went looking for the cantina.

Riding down a narrow dusty street, a flash of bright light flitted across his eyes. He glanced to his right to see what caused it. A tall brunette stood watching him through the partly opened door of a hovel. She held an open silver compact at her face. The sun had apparently reflected off the gleaming lid.

He started to speak and tell her it was safe to come out, but before he could, the woman drew back and shut the door.

⊘ **SIGNET** (0451)

# JON SHARPE'S WILD WEST

☐ **CANYON O'GRADY #1: DEAD MEN'S TRAILS by Jon Sharpe.** Meet Canyon O'Grady, a government special agent whose only badge, as he rides the roughest trails in the West, is the colt in his holster. O'Grady quickly learns that dead men tell no tales, and live killers show no mercy as he hunts down the slayer of the great American hero Merriwether Lewis. (160681—$2.95)

☐ **CANYON O'GRADY #2: SILVER SLAUGHTER by Jon Sharpe.** With a flashing grin and a blazing gun, Canyon O'Grady rides the trail of treachery, greed, and gore in search of nameless thieves who are stealing a vital stream of silver bullion from the U.S. government. (160703—$2.95)

☐ **CANYON O'GRADY #3: MACHINE GUN MADNESS by Jon Sharpe.** A gun was invented that spat out bullets faster than a man could blink and every malcontent in the Union wanted it. Canyon's job was to ride the most savage crossfire the West had ever seen to rescue the deadliest weapon the world had ever known. (161521—$2.95)

☐ **CANYON O'GRADY #4: SHADOW GUNS by Jon Sharpe.** With America split between North and South and Missouri being a border state both sides wanted, Canyon O'Grady finds himself in a crossfire of doublecross trying to keep a ruthless pro-slavery candidate from using bullets to win a vital election. (162765—$3.50)

☐ **CANYON O'GRADY #5: THE LINCOLN ASSIGNMENT by Jon Sharpe.** Bullets, not ballots, were Canyon O'Grady's business as top frontier trouble-shooter for the U.S. Government. But now he was tangled up in election intrigue, as he tried to stop a plot aimed at keeping Abe Lincoln out of office by putting him in his grave. (163680—$3.50)

---

Buy them at your local bookstore or use this convenient coupon for ordering.
NEW AMERICAN LIBRARY
P.O. Box 999, Bergenfield, New Jersey 07621

Please send me the books I have checked above. I am enclosing $_____ (please add $1.00 to this order to cover postage and handling). Send check or money order—no cash or C.O.D.'s. Prices and numbers are subject to change without notice.

Name_____

Address_____

City _____ State _____ Zip _____
Allow 4-6 weeks for delivery.
This offer, prices and numbers are subject to change without notice.

## Ⓢ SIGNET                                                      (0451)

# SWEEPING SAGAS FROM MATT BRAUN

☐ **THE SAVAGE LAND by Matt Braun.** Courage, passion, violence—in a surging novel of a Texas dynasty. The Olivers. Together they carved out an empire of wealth and power with sweat, blood, bravery and bullets.... (157214—$4.50)

☐ **EL PASO by Matt Braun.** El Paso was the wildest town in untamed Texas after the Civil War. Here men came with dreams of empire, and women with hopes of a better life on a virgin frontier. But Dallas Stoudenmire came to El Paso for a different reason—to end the reign of terror of the two vicious Banning brothers. In a town where his first mistake would be his last, Dallas was walking a tightrope.... (158430—3.50)

☐ **BUCK COLTER by Matt Braun.** Ruthless rancher Colonel John Covington wasn't about to let Buck Colter put down stakes and graze his herd on the open range he hogged for himself. But Colter had ideas of his own—mainly a blood score to settle with Covington. (161556—$3.50)

☐ **CIMARRON JORDAN by Matt Braun.** No man could match Cimarron Jordan's daring and only one could match his gun ... as he followed the thunder of buffalo, the roar of rifles, and the war cries of savage Indian tribes across the great Western Plains. (160126—$3.95)

**Buy them at your local**

**bookstore or use coupon**

**on next page for ordering.**

① SIGNET                                                    (0451)

# F.M. PARKER CORRALS THE WILD WEST

☐ **THE SHADOW MAN.** Jacob Tamarron arrives in Santa Fe just as war between Mexico and Texas breaks out. His beautiful new wife, Petra, vanishes in the raid of her family ranch by marauding bandits, driving him to hunt down the men responsible. "Absorbing, swift, action-packed!"—*Library Journal*                    (163869—$3.95)

☐ **THE FAR BATTLEGROUND** 1847. The Mexican War. They were men of conviction who fought for their country without fear, two soldiers, bound together by more than professional comraderie. Each owed the other his life. But now both men are thrust into a painful confrontation that tests the bounds of their loyalty and trust....          (156757—$3.50)

☐ **COLDIRON** It took a man as hard as cold-forged steel to carve himself a sprawling ranch out of the wilderness. Luke Coldiron's killer instinct lay dormant a long time, but now his kingdom is threatened by a private army of hand-picked murderers, and he has to find out whether he still has what it takes to survive....                (155726—$2.95)

☐ **SHADOW OF THE WOLF** Left for dead by a vicious army deserter and a renegade Indian warrior, Luke Coldiron fought his way back to the world of the living. Now he's coming after his foes ... ready to ride through the jaws of hell if he can blast them into it....          (155734—$2.95)

☐ **THE HIGHBINDERS.** A brutal gang of outlaws was out for miner's gold, and young Tom Galletin stood alone against the killing crew ... until he found an ally named Pak Ho. The odds were against them, but with Galletin's flaming Colt .45 and Pak Ho's razor-sharp, double-edged sword it was a mistake to count them out....          (155742—$2.95)

☐ **THE SHANGHAIERS** Young Tom Galletin had learned early to kill to survive in a land where the slow died fast. Luke Coldiron was a frontier legend among men who lived or died by their guns. Together they face the most vicious gang that ever traded human flesh for gold—and it looks like a fight to the death....                (151836—$2.95)

---

Buy them at your local bookstore or use this convenient coupon for ordering.

**NEW AMERICAN LIBRARY**
**P.O. Box 999, Bergenfield, New Jersey 07621**

Please send me the books I have checked above. I am enclosing $_____
(please add $1.00 to this order to cover postage and handling). Send check or money order—no cash or C.O.D.'s. Prices and numbers are subject to change without notice.

Name_____

Address_____

City _____ State _____ Zip Code _____
Allow 4-6 weeks for delivery.
This offer is subject to withdrawal without notice.

# 27 million Americans can't read a bedtime story to a child.

It's because 27 million adults in this country simply can't read.

Functional illiteracy has reached one out of five Americans. It robs them of even the simplest of human pleasures, like reading a fairy tale to a child.

You can change all this by joining the fight against illiteracy.

Call the Coalition for Literacy at toll-free **1-800-228-8813** and volunteer.

## Volunteer Against Illiteracy.
### The only degree you need is a degree of caring.

THIS AD PRODUCED BY MARTIN LITHOGRAPHERS
*A MARTIN COMMUNICATIONS COMPANY*